STAFF
NURSE

by

Lucy Agnes Hancock

WILDSIDE PRESS

CHAPTER ONE

JUDITH MORLEY GAZED at the petulant face on the pillow with mixed feelings. Angela Stacy was to have a tonsillectomy within the hour. Such a pretty girl—small, eighteen and spoiled. Now she was dramatizing the situation. Her big blue eyes were tragic, her pouting, unpainted mouth giving her the appearance of a sulky child. She had sent her long-suffering mother on some quite unnecessary errand and now turned to Judith with the demand:

"Just how good a sport are you, Nurse?"

"Why—that depends on what you might call sporting, Miss Stacy," Judith replied cautiously.

"Don't quibble," the girl said impatiently. "For Pete's sake, unbend. Forget you're on duty. Be a contemporary —an equal for a sec. Now, don't get up on your hind legs," as Judith stiffened. "I only meant be yourself— human."

Judith caught her breath then unexpectedly smiled into the stormy blue eyes. "Shoot!" she said.

"Get a pad and take this down," Angela ordered.

"Not making a will?" the nurse murmured. "Really you have nothing to fear. Doctor Cranford——"

"I know, I know," the girl interrupted. "Only scram— get that paper and write what I tell you before Mother gets back."

Judith picked up her notebook and stood at attention beside the bed, her pen poised ready for the message. Her gray eyes were quizzical and her lips twisted as she tried to repress a smile at the urgency in the other's face.

"I want you to telephone this message to Rufe—Rufus Grant—one-four-seven-one, in half an hour. You must begin by saying: 'This is Cranford Memorial Hospital calling for Angela Stacy.' Got that?" And at Judith's nod she went on: " 'The operation takes place in fifteen minutes and Miss Stacy wishes me to tell you good-bye and she is sorry for everything.' Then you are to ring off at once—

before he gets a chance to say anything. That'll hold him for a while. But be sure you get Rufe, himself."

"But—but Miss Stacy," Judith protested, "this is very misleading——"

"That's what it's intended to be," the young lady answered grimly. "Will you do it? Say so if you will. After all, it isn't your affair—and—you're being paid to take care of me." Her arrogance dropped for a moment as she put out her hand. "Please, Nurse. It means so much to me. Be a good scout and do it. Gosh! The parent's returning already!" She lowered her voice to a mere whisper. "If you breathe a word of this to anyone I'll—I'll die and haunt you all the rest of your life." Her eyes sparkled and her voice, while low, was menacing.

Judith laughed softly and patted the hand outside the coverlet. What an infant this Angela Stacy was! Against her saner judgment Judith nodded. It could do no harm —at least, she hoped it couldn't. Mrs. Stacy had entered, a huge bouquet in her arms. She came over to the bed and held the flowers at arm's length.

"Look, baby. Aren't they lovely? I found them in the shop around the corner. I think there's something so stimulating about the first spring flowers even if they are quite ahead of schedule. Don't you, Nurse?"

Judith assured her she did and left the room for a vase and water. Mrs. Stacy arranged the flowers, hands fluttery and head tipped first to left then right to get the desired effect. Angela frowned and muttered that she wished she would stop her everlasting fussing. Her mother seemed not to hear.

"I'll put them right where you can see them when you wake up after the operation, darling," she told her. "I'll be right here, too." She was brightly conversational although Judith knew she was frightened and worried.

"Why don't you go home, Mother?" Angela asked. "You can't do anything and—well—I'll be all right. Miss Morley will call you when it's all over——"

Her mother caught her breath. "No—no, indeed. I

4

wouldn't dream of leaving you. I shall stay right here with you, baby. I—I couldn't—simply couldn't leave you to go through this alone. How can you even suggest such a thing?"

"But it—it isn't much—anything to have one's tonsils out, Mother—just nothing at all. I wish you'd go home. You make me nervous," the girl said petulantly.

Mrs. Stacy's eyes filled with tears. "Don't ask me to leave you, darling," she pleaded. "I should never forgive myself—your father would never forgive me—I'll just sit over here in the corner and concentrate. After all, one must create a healing—a wholesome atmosphere———"

"Okay—okay," her daughter interrupted rudely, "only concentrate to yourself. I'm sorry," she went on, a note of apology creeping into her petulance. "I'm just jittery, I guess,, and you do fuss so—honestly, you do."

Her eyes ordered the nurse to be on her way to the telephone. Judith moved toward the door.

"Where are you going, Nurse?" Mrs. Stacy demanded, her voice panicky.

"Just down the hall, Mrs. Stacy. I won't be a minute. I'm going to give our patient something to quiet her. I'll be right back." She looked at her watch. "Just relax," she counseled both as she closed the door behind her.

At the telephone she dialed the number Angela Stacy had given her and asked to speak with Rufus Grant. In a minute a man's voice advised her that Rufus Grant was speaking. Judith delivered the message and replaced the instrument immediately but not before she heard a muttered imprecation. Smiling involuntarily, she turned to confront young Doctor Booth, who caught her hand in a close grip.

"Aha, me proud beauty," he chided in mock jealousy. "Caught in the act. I demand to know my rival's name. Tell me this instant and I shall do some expert carving on him."

Judith laughed softly. "Save your histrionics, you poor ham," she told him, extricating her hand and clasping it with the other one behind her back. "I'm merely Cupid's emissary."

The young interne relaxed visibly and let out an exaggerated sigh of relief. "Whose ruffled plumage are you smoothing at the moment, Judy? Not the Stacy brat?" At Judith's nod, he went on as if she had not answered, his dark eyes devouring her fresh, serene beauty. "What a wife you're going to make," he whispered.

Judith shook her head emphatically. "Don't be foolish, Larry."

"Foolish," she calls it," the young man complained to the empty corridor. "Here I'm wearing my heart on my sleeve and she refuses to give me so much as a word of encouragement. Now I ask you, is that the right way to treat a suitor for her hand and heart?"

Judith frowned although her pulses raced. She liked him very much, but after all he was almost too popular. She was afraid to trust either him or herself. Even when he singled her out for attention—seeming oblivious of the others—she held him off. Fear—an inhibition fostered in childhood from which she seemed unable to free herself— kept her from taking him at face value—believing his protestations. Maybe it was silly of her to be so meticulous in obeying the hospital's strict rules when she considered them not only far too stringent but provocative as well Larry insisted rules were made to be broken and the one forbidding nurses from having any social intercourse whatsoever with the male members of the staff was altogether wrong—inhuman in his opinion. And he refused to consider them applicable to him, anyway.

Lately, however, Judith had yielded to his urging. They had met at the public library and she had her first taste of unrestricted and unsupervised freedom. It was only after she was back in her room that grave doubts of the wisdom of her action assailed her and she had promised herself there would be no repetition. Hadn't Aunt Hepsie repeatedly warned her against men, especially handsome ones? And, certainly, Larry Booth was the best-looking

6

man she had ever known. She liked him—she said it over and over to herself, firmly and convincingly; but the old feeling of fear dampened her flaming spirits and took all the joy out of the escapade.

Since that first night, she had gone dancing with him on other occasions and each time the old doubts assailed her but a little less persistently. Was she growing hard and callous in wrongdoing as Aunt Hepsie declared her lovely mother had? Was it actually wrong to accept Larry's invitations? She was entitled to some fun, wasn't she? There had been precious little of it in her life so far. It couldn't be so very terrible because Doctor Cranford was inclined to be lenient with his staff. It was the superintendent, Miss Winters, who demanded obedience in every smallest detail.

None of the staff liked Miss Winters. Judith had tried but could not get through the icy wall of reserve that kept everyone at arm's length. She wondered if perhaps the superintendent's childhood had paralleled her own. Maybe she, too, had grown up in a house devoid of love and beauty. Maybe she couldn't break through and escape into the broader, happier life as Judith, by the grace of God and Doctor Wales, had been able to do.

As she stood before Doctor Booth in the empty corridor this morning, some of this flashed through Judith's mind. He had recaptured one of her hands and she found it hard to be stern while his touch was sending little waves of ecstasy up her arm to her heart. Now she attempted to withdraw her hand but he held it firmly, giving it a little shake in protest.

"Listen, Doctor Booth," Judith said as severely as she could. "This is neither the time nor the place for a flirtation. I'm on duty and 310 is due in the operating room in less than twenty minutes."

"How about tonight, beautiful? I know it's your late night. I've been keeping tabs on you. Let's go over to the big town for dinner and dancing. I've a windfall and need someone to help me spend it. Can do?" His eyes

7

were compelling—dark and long-lashed, they said things to her—things at once thrilling and frightening. Larry certainly had a way with him.

Down at the end of the corridor the elevator whirred and Judith drew back from his detaining hand. "Okay. I'll meet you at Drakes'. I have to get tooth paste."

He stood his ground. "Early, Judy," he urged. "Eight— no later. I'll be waiting—with Bill's coupé. See you then, dar-ling," he whispered as the elevator slid to a stop and two nurses stepped from the car. He paused to chat with them for a moment and Judith frowned as she heard their low laughter. That was the trouble with Larry. He was all things to all girls. Unreliable. Not a man to tie to, and yet she was afraid she was beginning to love him. Aunt Hepsie's piercing black eyes and sharp voice came to her.

"They'll try to get you with soft words an' tender glances, Judy; but don't you ever put any trust in 'em. Remember what happened to your mother. Don't forget what your father did to her before you were born. Don't you ever forget the life your mother lived—a disgrace to her sex. You're the spittin' image of her an' if you don't watch out you'll follow in her footsteps. Men ain't to be trusted, girl. They're live ravenin' wolves. They been the curse of Leeds women for generations. Men!" She spat the word with venom, and the little girl had cowered before her. Only once had she dared remind the old woman that her father had been killed while looking for work and that her mother was beautiful and sweet and she loved her. On that occasion her aunt had driven her from the room for daring to talk back. Now with a gesture of impatience she banished the vision.

Back in 310 she encountered questioning blue eyes and nodded. The girl relaxed and Judith wondered how a man with the slow, deep, decidedly mature voice of Rufus Grant could have become mixed up with the spoiled little chit before her.

8

"Well?" Angela asked, frowning in the direction of her mother's pale, worried face near the window.

"Everything according to schedule," Judith reported, smiling.

"But——"

"No," Judith assured her. "Nothing. As you requested, I didn't give him a chance."

"You were frightfully long," the girl complained and stared suspiciously at Judith's sudden blush.

"One of the doctors stopped me for a moment," she explained. Then, to halt further questioning she went on: "Now this won't hurt at all." She used a bit of alcohol-moistened cotton on Angela's slim white arm and injected the hypodermic.

"Ouch!" muttered the girl and her mother gasped, her eyes wide with terror.

"O-oh!" she breathed.

"For gosh sake, look at Mother!" Angela cried in disgust. "She's passed out. Can you tie that? She's a bigger baby than I am. She faints at the drop of a hat."

However, the faint was of short duration and as she sipped the cold water Judith brought her, Mrs. Stacy apologized for being so silly. But she was shaken and Judith felt sorry for her. Angela grew drowsy and it wasn't long until the stretcher arrived and she was wheeled from the room.

It was less than an hour later that Rufus Grant entered the gray stone walls of Cranford Memorial Hospital and asked to be directed to the room occupied by Miss Angela Stacy. He was given the necessary information but told he would not be allowed to see her.

Outside 310 he encountered Angela's mother hurrying to the telephone to report the result of the operation to her husband. She stared at the tall, red-haired young man through tear-dimmed eyes. He caught her hands in his.

"What is it, Mrs. Stacy? An accident?"

Mrs. Stacy shook her head. Tears streamed down her cheeks, leaving her face shiny and streaked.

"What is it? Is it over? Will she live?"

"Yes," the woman choked. "But she's still unconscious. And she's so—s-sick—so terribly sick!"

"I'm sorry," the man murmured. "Just what was the matter?"

"Her—her tonsils," Mrs. Stacy gulped, wiping her eyes.

The man gasped, swallowed with difficulty and struggled to hide a grin. "But—but it's nothing serious, is it?" he managed.

"That's what the doctor's say," Angela's mother retorted indignantly. "A lot they know about it. She might have died. And she's all we have. I've been so frightened——"

"I'm sure you have; but she will be all right. I came in place of Rufe. He's gone on a fishing trip with the Townsend boys. Of course he would have come himself if he had been here. Is there anything I can do?"

Judith came into the corridor. Mrs. Stacy caught her hand. "How is she?"

"All right. Please don't worry about her, Mrs. Stacy," Judith said, wondering who the man was.

"This is Mr. Grant, Miss Morley—Angela's nurse—Miss Morley—Mr. Grant," she flustered. "Oh, you talk to him, Nurse. I—I can't. I must telephone Richard. Poor baby, she's so frightfully ill!" She hurried away to the nearest telephone.

The tall young man grinned down at the slender, gray-eyed girl in white and Judith frowned. After all, Angela *was* pretty sick just now and her parents were scared to death. Pray why should this debonair stranger think it all such a joke? She would like to tell him that having that awful fire in one's throat wasn't exactly pleasant nor was the nausea occasioned by the anesthetic. But of course she couldn't do that. He was supposed to think the operation a major one and be extremely anxious. Anxious! Not this conceited male standing before her with a knowing smirk on his good-looking face. He made her sick.

"I take it you are Mr. Rufus Grant?" Judith asked coolly. "Well, you can't see Miss Stacy this morning. She won't be entirely out of ether before evening and even then she should not have visitors. Complete rest and quiet are indicated." She had to say that for the girl's sake.

"I haven't the least intention of intruding, Miss—Miss Morley," he assured her pleasantly. "I merely dropped by to inquire if there is anything I can do to help. You see, the telephone message was very misleading." So he knew. Mrs. Stacy must have told him. Poor Angela!

The young man went on talking. "I didn't know what to think but if she is going to be all right—well, isn't there something I can do to brighten her stay here?"

"I'm sure I wouldn't know," Judith replied, refusing to unbend. "Perhaps her mother——"

"Oh, I tried to talk to her. She's too jittery to tell me anything."

What on earth can a man of—thirty maybe—he must be nearly that—have in common with childish eighteen-year-old Angela Stacy? Judith asked herself. Cradle-snatcher! she jeered mentally. He was gazing at her, questioning yet amused. His brown eyes twinkled and his lips twitched as if he found the whole affair most diverting.

"I'm afraid you will have to decide that for yourself then," the girl told him and turned to re-enter the room. "I'll tell Miss Stacy you called, Mr.—Mr. Grant, when she shows signs of becoming interested in the doings of her friends." She opened the door of 310.

"Wait," the man pleaded but the door closed firmly. Rufus Grant stared at the white panels and wondered what he could have said or done to be so summarily dismissed.

It was mid-afternoon before Angela Stacy became aware of her surroundings. Rufus Grant had evidently decided on plenty of roses, for a great basket of American Beauties had arrived just before noon. Two hours later, a five-pound box of candy was delivered at the door of 310. The card accompanying it was what Judith described to herself as positively maudlin. Mrs. Stacy smiled approvingly as she read it and handed it over to Judith.

11

"He's really very thoughtful, isn't he?" she murmured. "Angela will be so proud and happy!"

And a bit later, Angela became big-eyed and ecstatic as she pressed the card to her heart. At four came a huge basket of fruit all done up in cellophane and yards of pink satin ribbon and as she gazed at the card bearing the words: "Chin up. Love. Rufe," she wept weakly but happily.

Mrs. Stacy rushed over to the bed and patted her daughter's shoulder, purring and murmuring like a mother cat. Judith bathed the girl's flushed face and brushed the soft yellow hair, tying it back with the wide blue ribbon her mother had brought. Angela's eyes met those of the nurse. They said plainly: "Now aren't you glad you telephoned? You see?"

Judith smiled and nodded understandingly although it was her own private opinion that Rufus Grant was overdoing it a bit. Was this lavish attention to be continued for the entire week? It was at five that Judith suggested Mrs. Stacy go out for a brief walk. Angela nodded approval of the idea.

"I'll go meet your father, baby," the lady agreed somewhat reluctantly. "You're sure she will be all right?" she asked.

"Of course," Judith assured her while Angela made a grimace of exasperation.

"Well then, we'll have dinner downtown and be back before seven." She stooped to kiss her daughter, lingering broodingly for a moment then hurried away, her eyes moist.

"Mother's a goon," Angela muttered disrespectfully.

"She's sweet," Judith protested. She felt a wave of nostalgia as a fleeting picture came to her of her own mother bending over her cot when she had the measles. It was gone in a flash, blotted out by the vision of Aunt Hepsie's bitter face as she warned her that only the strong survived in this selfish, wicked world. Her parents were weaklings—the world was no place for them. Judith didn't agree with Aunt Hepsie. Even as a child something deep within her shrank from accepting the old woman's warped

12

philosophy; but it had succeeded in dimming and blurring memories of her mother that the girl would gladly have kept fresh and green.

"Sure," Angela agreed, "but a goon just the same." She made a wry face and clutched her throat.

"Don't try to talk for a while," Judith advised. "The soreness will soon pass—all the quicker if you're quiet."

The lovely lips pouted for a moment then she re-read her cards and smiled beatifically.

It was just before Judith went off duty at seven that a telegram was delivered at 310. Angela was feeling much better although she still complained bitterly of her throat, the fact that she was hungry and couldn't eat and that visitors were barred. She tore open the envelope and stared at the message with unbelieving, dilated eyes then thrust it out to Judith.

"You said——" she began accusingly. Then, tragically, waving a deprecating hand to include flowers, candy and fruit: "Take them away! Throw 'em in the rubbish can. Burn 'em—anything—only get them out of here. I hate everything in this room. I'll—I'll——"

The message read: "JUST HEARD ADVISE AMPUTATION OF TEMPER CAUGHT THREE BEAUTIES CHIN UP.

(Signed) RUFE."

Angry tears were streaming down Angela's cheeks when her mother and father entered the room a moment later. Judith was trying to soothe her, bathing her face and murmuring comforting platitudes although she was distinctly puzzled.

Mrs. Stacy exclaimed at her daughter's tears while the girl's father dropped to his knees beside the bed.

"What is it?" Mrs. Stacy looked accusingly at the nurse. Angela held out the crumpled telegram. "Why—why——" the lady stammered helplessly.

Mr. Stacy read it and laughed. "The young scalawag. His own temper isn't exactly beatific, is it, Angel? No, I should say not. So he's having good luck. Wish I could

13

get way for a few days' fishing. Nothing to weep over, baby," he soothed.

"But—but I thought the flowers and—and things were from h-him," she wept. "You told me he called," she accused the nurse.

"O-oh," her mother panted. "I thought I told you Rufe was away and that his uncle came in his place."

Angela glared at her mother through wet, stormy eyes. "You didn't and I—I've—I've been so hap-happy!"

"There, there," murmured her father, patting her cheek. "I bet a dollar to a new hat Rufe left word with his uncle to pinch-hit for him if the need arose. Rufe's a good lad, baby, and thinks the world of you."

Angela wiped her eyes, blew her nose on her father's spotless handkerchief and smiled into his anxious face.

"Maybe he does," she murmured, "but——"

"I wouldn't encourage her to talk tonight," Judith interrupted. "She will be better for remaining quiet."

The door opened and Marie Hood, the relief, entered. The Stacys had insisted on both a day and a night nurse and the best room available in the hospital for Angela's tonsillectomy. The best was none too good for their one wee lamb. Hood picked up the chart and over its meager recordings eyed the occupants of the room. She encountered the gray gaze of Judith Morley and followed her into the corridor.

"Say, what is this?" she asked. "From the looks of things in there one would think 310's death was imminent. Okay, isn't she?"

"Of course she is," Judith told her, "only she's all they have—the child of their old age, so to speak, and they worry if she breathes once too often. The girl doesn't help them any. She works on their sympathy to get her own way. She's spoiled and in love; but not too bad at that."

"I think I'll give the parents a hint to leave early, Morley," Hood said. "Doting parents can certainly play havoc with a patient's nerves not to mention those of the nurse. In my humble opinion, it would be lots better for all con-

14

cerned if evening visiting hours were cut out entirely. I
don't hold with 'em. Mm-mm," she muttered as the door
opened and Mr. Stacy came out with the fruit and candy.

"Oh-h," he exclaimed as he saw the two nurses standing
close by. "I was afraid you had gone, Miss—Miss—Nurse.
Angela wants you to have these. She says you forgot to
take them. Her mother and I have advised her to keep
the roses. After all, Rufus meant it kindly. You understand,
don't you? I'm sure you do." He thrust his burden into
Judith's reluctant arms and returned to his daughter.

"My word, what a break!" Hood cried as she examined
the elaborate wrappings. "Aren't you in luck! None of
my patients are so generous to me."

"I'll pass them on to Pediatrics," Judith said. "I'm sure
I don't want them."

"You're a nut!" the other exclaimed. "What ails you?
Is there by any chance poison in them that you turn up
your nose in refusal? If you don't want 'em—leave 'em
in my room. I'm not so finicky."

The whirr of the elevator reached them and Marie slipped back into 310 while Judith, laden with spoils, went
on down the corridor. She would deposit her burden in
the children's ward and then go on to her room to change
for her date with Larry. Her heartbeats quickened with
her step. She would wear her new spring hat. It was almost warm enough for her suit. Even if it was only March,
there was practically no snow and every indication of a
lovely night.

The elevator disgorged some half dozen people who
scattered in various directions and as Judith turned a corner of the long corridor she came face to face with Rufus
Grant. She blushed as she saw him glance quizzically at
the trophies she bore. He grinned down at her. Really he
must be over six feet—two or three at least. Judith had
always secretly admired tall men but suddenly she decided
he was far too tall. It gave him an unfair advantage.

"So Angela didn't like my choice of gifts," he said. "I

confess I'm a dud at such things, but I tried to put myself in Rufe's place."

"I'm taking them over to Pediatrics," Judith explained stiffly. "Miss Stacy felt it rather a pity to let them grow stale when the children will no doubt enjoy them." She took a step forward but he barred the way.

"The flowers were all right?" he asked.

"Evidently," Judith said.

The man stood for a moment as if trying to think of something that would prolong the conversation then asked quickly: "Did she hear directly from Rufe? I wired him."

"Yes," Judith told him. "She received a telegram this evening."

"I'm glad of that," he said. "Say—please don't think I'm fresh," he began diffidently, "but—are you off duty now? Will you go to dinner with me—and—and maybe a movie or something?"

"I'm sorry," Judith replied, still coolly, for somehow this man antagonized her. For some unknown reason she thoroughly disliked him. "I have an engagement."

"O-oh." He was patently disappointed. "I suppose you couldn't break it?" he asked tentatively, his brown eyes twinkling.

"I don't break engagements, Mr.—Mr.——" she said coldly, purposely leaving his name unuttered. Why, he seemed actually to find her amusing! How dared he?

"What? Never? Couldn't you make an exception in this one instance? You see, I'm leaving town tomorrow——"

"I don't break engagements, Mr. Grant," she insisted, having the grace to feel ashamed of her smugness. Her tone was definitely hostile. She was annoyed at herself for acting as she did but couldn't seem to help it. If only he wasn't so darned assured! It made her mad. Her head lifted haughtily. "Now if you will kindly allow me to pass——"

The young man stared at her for a long moment while his expression changed. His brown eyes darkened—the half-smile left his lips.

"Oh, I do most humbly beg your pardon, Lady Astor-bilt," he said ironically. "I assure you my intentions were entirely innocent. You must have had some unfortunate experiences to resent—so intensely—my perfectly harmless and friendly overtures." He drew himself to his full height, bowed low and waved a hand toward the now deserted corridor. "Pass, Duchess!" he burlesqued. "The whole world is yours, quite free from further advances from Rufus Grant."

"Swell!" exclaimed Judith as the young man, his back very straight, stalked away toward room 310. Suddenly she smiled and felt an urge to call to him—to apologize—to tell him she wasn't really one bit like she seemed; but quickly smothered it. He was insufferable—conceited and like all that wealthy set, an irresponsible playboy. She wanted none of them. She wondered vaguely how it was that the old feeling of inferiority—the fear and dread that so often possessed her when talking with young men—had been absent in this case. Suddenly she felt free—buoyant, alive and young. What was there to be afraid of? Going about with Larry had done wonders to help dislodge her old man of the sea. Aunt Hepsie was wrong—so terribly wrong—or maybe she was right. Maybe Judith Morley, R.N., was strong. Maybe she was the one to remove the curse Aunt Hepsie insisted dogged all Leeds women. Perhaps deep within her was the power to withstand temptation—to keep men in their rightful place—outside her orbit of living. But her smile was rueful as she went on to her room in the nurses' home. Her brief taste of popularity with the male sex had been sweet. She didn't want to go back into her shell—at least not just yet.

CHAPTER TWO

JUDITH NEVER KNEW her father. He disappeared before she was born. Killed, her mother insisted—killed and lying somewhere in an unmarked grave. But Aunt Hepsie stoutly maintained it was a plain case of desertion and only what one was to expect after Alice Leeds had made a runaway match with a boy no one knew. Jude Morley, he had called himself, but the old woman didn't believe it was his name. Judith's mother had told her he was "big and handsome and sweet." Aunt Hepsie declared he was no account. There was no photograph of him so Judith used to make up pictures of him. Her mother had given her two small willow whistles Jude had made on their brief honeymoon. Judith treasured them as the one link she had with her father. Aunt Hepsie contended that was all he was good for—a trifling, shiftless, lazy good-for-nothing. But if there was no likeness of her father available, the pictures of her mother, grave and gay, subdued and reckless but always young and lovely, passed in kaleidoscope review before her eyes. She had adored her mother.

When Judith was eight, Alice Morley was killed in a motor accident and people said, as they will when the picture is incomplete or blurred—when they are only too eager to believe the worst—that she got just what she deserved and Jason Barnes, too, although they felt sorry for his poor wife and family. Judith had set her firm little jaw and defied the world. From that time on, the fate of Alice Morley was a dire warning held before the girls of Niles Corners and vicinity.

Old Aunt Hepsie declared it was only what one could expect from the trash living in the village. She had never neighbored and never would. Her dilapidated cottage was nearly a quarter of a mile from the nearest house. Three girls lived there, the youngest about Judith's age. But the children never played with her. She walked the mile to and from school alone.

After her mother's death, Judith was kept far too busy

helping in the house and garden to have time to play and she grew up a lonely, shy, unfriendly girl. Many times her aunt planned to keep her at home—cut her education short. Aunt Hepsie could see no sense in submitting the child to a continuation of snubbing and ridicule. But the "nosey riffraff" saw to it that the plan wasn't put into operation. Judith went to school, through primary grades to grammar and on by bus to high school in Medford. She would graduate with her class even if she wasn't of it.

Judith was quite aware that she was different and she prepared for the ordeal of graduation with dread. She knew she would be all wrong. Her dress, an old white one of her mother's, inexpertly adjusted to her smaller frame, was bound to look queer. The white satin slippers, sizes too large and insecurely kept on by means of pasteboard insoles, were uncomfortable. The heavy dark braids wound around her head, because Aunt Hepsie wouldn't allow her to cut them off, added years to her age, and her hands, rough and red from working in the garden, proclaimed her a drudge and contributed to the sullen resentment she felt at being compelled to be present at all. She wished she might get sick and so have an excuse for staying home; but she had never been sick in her life except when she had the measles. It was nothing new for her to be ignored; but on commencement night, with her classmates wearing delectable white frocks of organdy or some other thin material; with their short hair curling about their excited faces, she feared her throat would burst with envy and despair.

"Don't be a weakling, child," Aunt Hepsie had admonished her in the fierce, bitter voice that was habitual with her. "You've got a bad heritage to be sure; but you can pull through if you only keep your head and use what brains you've got. You ain't bad looking even though you ain't specially brilliant. And you've got guts. That's more'n either your mother or father had. He couldn't get a job and your mother had too many—now, now, none of your sass, young lady," as Judith's eyes glowed indignantly and

19

her mouth opened to deny the allegation. "I know what I'm talkin' about and you mind your manners—if you've got any. Don't let anyone get the best of you. Understand? You've got a lot to live down but you've got spunk and you ain't lazy. That's due to me though I don't expect to get any thanks for it."

Judith had heard much the same thing many times before and resented it with every fibre of her being. No one could ever convince her that her pretty, gay young mother was bad. How could she have been when she was always so sweet and kind to her? When she came back to the cottage after a hard day at the Jason Barnes insurance office in Medford to bake and clean, wash and iron and even help in the garden where to the child's admiring eyes she was something extra special because she wore gloves and a huge sunhat. No one else in Niles Corners wore gloves to garden. Aunt Hepsie called it being tony—putting on airs; but to Judith it was wonderful.

As Judith looked back on that horrible night of her graduation she smiled wryly though tears stung her eyelids in pity for the defiant young thing that had been Judith Morley. She recalled leaving the house and hurrying along the path to the corner where the school bus was to pick her up and carry her to the high school in Medford. She slipped out of her heavy oxfords, hid them behind a stone wall. and put on the white slippers. She wasn't a minute too soon. The bus driver stared for a moment then grinned in friendly fashion. Judith flushed scarlet. He had never noticed her before. It must be that he hadn't recognized her. A little wave of relief eased the pain in her heart. Maybe she looked all right. She smoothed the skirt of the white dress she wore and lifted shy eyes to her fellow passengers. They didn't seem to be paying any attention to her and she breathed easier.

"You look right nice," Aunt Hepsie had said as she viewed the result of her grandniece's toilet. "Now just remember to walk careful—don't race like you thought the old boy himself was after you or you had to catch a train somewheres. Try to act like you were just as good as the rest of 'em. Here, let me hold that glass. First thing you know you'll drop it and it's a sure thing we don't want seven more years' bad luck." She shifted the mirror by slow degrees so that Judith could see, piecemeal, her entire length. It wasn't so bad.

As the bus rumbled through the village and out into the country again, Judith's thought flew ahead to the big, sprawling red brick building which was the pride of Medford. Her very soul shrank from the ordeal before her. It might not have been so bad if Olive Barnes had graduated with her own class instead of flunking out and joining this one. Suddenly Judith's head lifted. It was only for tonight. After tonight she would be free from her tormenters forever. Some of the load slipped from her heart. A woman across the aisle turned and smilingly asked:

"Are you in the graduating class, my dear?"

Judith gulped in astonishment and nodded, the smile coming a little late. Maybe it was a good omen. Perhaps it wouldn't be so awful after all; but she said it without conviction.

The bus stopped in front of the high school and Judith followed the other passengers up the wide cement walk to the entrance. There, she left them and went carefully on to the science room where the class was to form in line for the march to Assembly. She paused outside the door, her heart sinking. Suppressed laughter and the shifting of restless feet made her draw back in panic. She heard the orchestra playing and knew the time was short. She must go in and find her place. Stifling her terror she entered, not with the proudly lifted head and assured manner she had promised herself; but shyly, almost fearfully while her classmates, gathered in little groups of threes and fours, drew closer together and stared. She made no effort to join them but found a place near the wall and waited for the signal to form in line.

Miss Soule, the English teacher, entered hurriedly. Her sharp eyes scanned the room. She patted a shoulder here and there, smiled at one or two of her favorites and raised her hands for silence. Judith felt her roving glance reach her, pause for a moment and then almost too quickly pass on around the room. Judith didn't like Miss Soule. Suddenly a numbness assailed her, making her indifferent to the opinion of the others. What was it to her that the girls all looked like pictures in a magazine—that the boys in their immaculate white pants and dark coats were now even more fearsome than ever? They couldn't hurt her. Let them stare—let them nudge each other. She didn't care—but she did.

The signal was given. The class formed ready for the march along the hall to Assembly. Miss Soule stood aside, a set smile on her thin, hawklike face. Judith walked beside tall, gangling Jerome Mettlach, the school joke, who despised girls and insulted anyone who attempted to make friends with him. Judith ignored him. She kept step until they parted at the fourth row of reserved seats, Jerome going one way and Judith the other. Her strangely defiant pride held until she received her diploma and stepped back. Then catastrophe! The heel of one ill-fitting slipper caught on a corner of the rug. She stumbled. The slipper flew off, disclosing the brown pasteboard insoles to the goggling eyes of her classmates. Perhaps she only imagined it; but there was an interminable pause while she righted herself, slipped into her shoe and took her place at the end of the row of girls.

Shame and horror enveloped her. She was all wrong. Her dress was wrong, her slippers were wrong, her hair was wrong. She was queer—awkward, clumsy, different from the others. She hated them all, herself included.

Judith knew nothing of the rest of the program. She sensed rather than saw that a black-coated man stepped to the front of the rostrum and raised his hands. The benediction. It was over. The graduating class swarmed from the platform to the assembly floor to be immediately surrounded by admiring parents and teachers, relatives and friends. No one noticed Judith as she slipped from the room and ran down the stairs and into the soft darkness of the June night.

The bus was parked near the corner and she climbed aboard. The driver hadn't yet appeared. Judith was glad to be alone with her hot cheeks, her shame and her hatred. Her diploma was clutched tightly in one hand. She held it at arm's length, staring at it with hard gray eyes. It had cost her plenty—more than it was worth. She felt she wanted nothing so much as to creep into the house and up to her room to bury her head in her pillow and forget the hurt and humiliation of this horrible night.

The following August, Aunt Hepsie suffered a stroke and lingered for two months completely helpless. It was then that Judith came to know the meaning of neighbors. Aunt Hepsie could no longer forbid them the house and Judith was too tired, too harried and too frightened to want to. But it was hard for her to accept help and there were times, while Aunt Hepsie lay and muttered meaninglessly, that she wished these well-meaning women would go and leave her alone. But they didn't and when one night Aunt Hepsie died in her sleep, the neighbors took complete charge. It seemed as if they were satisfying a long cherished desire to do things for one who had held them up to scorn and derision; who had refused their offers of friendship and help. They seemed to find pleasure in taking things into their own hands. Judith resented it but she was helpless. Doctor Wales, the only man Aunt Hepsie considered fit to live, prescribed a mild sedative and gave orders to put Judith to bed. Against her will the girl submitted. She slept the clock around.

She awoke to find the cottage scoured from attic to cellar. The pantry was suddenly overflowing with food. Someone brought her a black dress and her first pair of kid pumps. From somewhere there appeared a black coat, hat, gloves and accessories. Judith shrank with wounded pride yet was powerless to refuse such obvious kindness. It was as if the pent-up neighborliness of years had at last burst its dam to overwhelm her.

It puzzled Judith that Aunt Hepsie's funeral should be so largely attended; the flowers so profuse. Not only garden flowers that the neighbors had protected from frost; but wreaths and crosses and crescents of hothouse blooms. In life Aunt Hepsie had been a recluse—an unapproachable, disagreeable one at that. Why all this fuss after she was dead? She couldn't understand it. It savored of show —of hypocrisy—to the girl. She stood beside the grave of the strange, forbidding old woman who had so grudgingly given her food and shelter, and wept, not in sorrow at her passing, but from bitter loneliness. While Aunt Hepsie lived Judith felt she was needed—she had work to do. Now there was no one—she had nothing.

The minister, a tall, somber man in shabby black, patted her shoulder, called her "my dear bereaved child," urged her to call on him if he could be of help and went his way. He was a busy man and Aunt Hepsie had countless times driven him from her premises. One or two of the women spoke to her and if Judith answered she didn't know it. She felt paralyzed. The driver of the automobile reserved for her drove her back to the cottage. Several cars were parked in the yard but she didn't see them. She went slowly up the path to the front door open to the autumn sunshine. Voices reached her. Oh, she wished they would go!

Dinner was on the table in the dining room. White-aproned women flew about serving the dozen or so men and women seated there. There was laughter and talk and Judith stood staring with unbelieving eyes until someone shushed sibilantly and silence fell. One of the white-aproned women pulled out a chair and invited Judith to sit down but the girl shook her head and climbed the stairs to her room. No one followed.

In time the house grew quiet. From her window she saw the last car drive away—the last aproned woman close the sagging gate and follow her husband down the path to the village. It was only then that she went downstairs.

24

All was in shining order. She wandered about, dazed and helpless. What was she to do now?

It was perhaps an hour later that a knock sounded on the door. Judith opened it to the family doctor. Doctor Wales was the only person in the world she felt she knew. Even Aunt Hepsie had nothing against him. Perhaps it was because of his rough, homely manner; his abrupt way of giving orders and expecting them to be obeyed. He was a tall, stoop-shouldered man, rugged and ungainly, with a large nose, keen blue eyes and a shaggy mane of white hair. Now he removed the raincoat he always wore regardless of the weather, draped it over the back of a chair, placed the battered black felt hat on top and followed Judith into the smaller parlor.

"Well, Judith, how goes it?" he asked, lowering his long length into the one easy chair the room afforded. "All right, are you?"

"Yes," Judith replied dully. "All right, I guess."

The doctor cleared his throat. "What you aimin' to do? Get you a job of some sort?"

"I—I suppose so," the girl answered.

"Got anything in mind? You could do housework— cookin' an' cleanin' an' such, but you don't want that. You've had enough o' that. D'you know, Judy, you'd make a crackerjack nurse," he told her. His eyes narrowed as he watched her reactions. "You've got the makin's. Ever thought about it?"

"But——" Judith paused. She couldn't tell him she didn't know how to go about becoming a nurse. She couldn't let him see how dumb she was.

"Well?" the doctor prodded. "But what?"

"Nothing."

"Sort of considerin' the money angle, ain't you? Listen. I need a girl in my office right now. You come work for me for a spell an' you'll earn enough money to get started, anyway. That is, if you aim to take a nursin' course. You're 'most eighteen—will be pretty soon, won't it?"

"In December," the girl said, trembling with a mixture of dread and excitement.

"I happen to know your school record's okay and I'm willin' to back you if you need backin'. You see, Judy, you'll get your keep while you're learnin' an' you'll be with young folks. That's what you need right now more'n anything else in the world. You been alone too much. Well?" he asked. "How does it sound to you?"

Judith looked into the kind blue eyes opposite her own and blinked rapidly. She wasn't used to such thoughtfulness. She must not cry. She must be hard and strong. The world had no place for weaklings. Hadn't Aunt Hepsie preached that to her ever since she was a baby? She swallowed the lump in her throat and took a long breath. It steadied her.

"I'll try awfully hard, Doctor Wales," she said gravely. "I don't know whether or not I will make a nurse; but I can try."

"That's the spirit!" he commended. "Want to get your doll rags an' come home with me right now? You can't stay here all by yourself an' Mis' Simpson'll make you right comfortable. She does me. It's quite a piece out to my place, you know, an' I'm on my way there this minute. Office hours from six to eight."

"But—but I can't——"

"Bosh!" the doctor exclaimed, sensing with uncanny insight the girl's hesitation to accept help. 'Mis' Simpson'll find ways to keep you busy when you ain't workin' for me, Judy. Trust her for that. She's a little like your Aunt Hepsie but not too much. Don't you worry for fear you won't earn your keep. My housekeeper an' I ain't as spry as we used to be an' can use a pair of young hands an' feet, not to mention eyes. This ain't charity, my child. I wouldn't insult a smart, up-an'-comin' girl like you by offerin' charity. Sometimes pride's about all a body's got. You keep yours, Judy. Keep your chin firm and your head high and your two feet on the ground and you'll make out. No, child, I ain't offerin' you charity. It's just good horse sense on my part. Hustle along now while I take a look around."

At the door Judith turned. "I suppose the sooner I leave here the better," she said tentatively.

"The better for you," the doctor told her bluntly. "An' take along everything that belongs to you. Tom Butler's married daughter's aimin' to move in tomorrow or next day. Accounts for all the housecleanin' an' disturbance you been endurin'. Tom's got a blanket mortgage on everything, you know, or don't you?"

"No," Judith replied. "I never knew any of Aunt Hepsie's business."

"Just as well," the doctor said. "She took care of everything an' her money lasted out her lifetime—that's all she wanted. You got to look out for yourself. Run along now."

"I haven't much to take of my own, Doctor Wales. I can take my mother's trunk, can't I? I'd like to."

"Don't see why not, if it ain't too cumbersome."

"Oh, it's just a small trunk. Maybe I can put my things in it, too. I won't be long."

Judith lived with Doctor Wales and his housekeeper until she entered the training school for nurses at Procton General Hospital the following February. During those months she made no friends. The repression of years could not be lightly shaken off, but she learned a great deal. She worked hard, never sparing herself, and came to understand and like Doctor Wales more and more each day. Mrs. Simpson was another matter. The housekeeper remembered Alice Morley and had known the Barnes family rather well, or so she intimated. She had encountered Aunt Hepsie but once and declared it more than sufficient. It was evident she didn't approve of the doctor's action in taking Judith into the house; but her displeasure didn't faze the doctor one bit. Judith didn't like her. She asked questions. Judith froze. Doctor Wales protested. Thereafter an armed truce prevailed between the housekeeper and Judith until the day she left for Procton. But though Mrs. Simpson didn't approve of Judith she knew her duty and did it by her. When Judith left for training school, her trunk and suitcase—purchased under the stern eye of the housekeeper —were filled with such things as the Doctor and Mrs. Simpson felt the girl needed. Nothing lavish but adequate. Judith, for the first time in her life, was well dressed and so felt inconspicuous—a comforting feeling for her.

At Procton, Judith proved herself a good student, a conscientious nurse. The faculty liked her; her fellow students not so well. The internes called her the "Snow Princess" and turned their attention to more responsive girls. The graduate nurses dubbed her the "Ice Cube" while the student nurses left her much to herself. Apparently Judith didn't mind. If at times she longed to enter into their fun, she gave no sign. She overheard one of the girls call her "high-hat" and smiled to herself. If they only knew! But they didn't. It wasn't until her senior year that she fell in love—with one of her patients.

Mrs. Roderick Leeds had come to the hospital for a rest. She was seventy-eight years old, a well-to-do, determined old lady, bent on getting the most out of life in spite of her frailties. In order to accomplish this she came to the hospital each year for a month of rest and treatment under the expert and affectionate eye of her friend, Doctor Horner, house physician at Procton General. Judith had heard of Mrs. Leeds but had never happened to see her until she entered her room on that mild evening in early April.

All her life, Mrs. Leeds had firmly believed that

"Early to bed and early to rise
Makes a man miss all the fun till he dies."

So she turned her night into day and Judith discovered the biggest part of her job was to entertain her patient. She found this hard work. She knew herself to be entirely inadequate as an entertainer and wished the superintendent had given the job of night duty in 717 to someone else.

For two or three nights Mrs. Leeds did most of the entertaining. She had been everywhere and seen everything and Judith listened enthralled. But one evening the old lady asked questions. Judith was reluctant to talk about herself. To her amazement and consternation she found the grim, sordid story of her childhood pouring from her lips.

"Why, my dear!" the old lady had exclaimed when the girl paused in her torrent of words to sit horror-stricken at what she had done. "This is Providence. I'm all stark alone in the world, too. Let's join forces. Shall we? At least for the month I shall remain here. I shall adore pretending you are my granddaughter."

"My mother's name was Leeds—Alice Leeds," Judith told her. "But she had no relatives except Aunt Hepsie."

"You have a lovely name, my dear. Judith. I always think of it as belonging to someone strong and brave and gracious."

It was amazing the way Judith blossomed under the loving, yet critical eye of her patient. Mrs. Leeds advised her about clothes, recommended her own beautician, urging the girl to put herself into Celestine's capable hands. Judith gave up her braids without regrets and felt herself to be a different person. Mrs. Leeds introduced her to Madame Bouvé who encouraged her to attend one of her private dancing classes. There Judith met girls and boys of her own age who were just as shy and backward in social accomplishments as she was herself. Life opened invitingly after that. She lost some of her feeling of inferiority, shyness and fear. When she left Procton to do general duty at Cranford Memorial in Nottingham, it was like beginning a new existence. She felt she was ready for friendship—ready to give it and to accept it. Brenda Newton and Isabelle Carey were the first friends she ever had.

It wasn't to be expected that the inhibitions of a suppressed girlhood could be sloughed easily. Judith continued to suffer spasms of fear and dread. There were times when she felt an impending doom—when she avoided the friendly overtures of her housemates and kept to herself. But she strove with these moods mightily and after a while occasionally accepted an invitation to the movies, to dine

29

and dance with one or another of Nottingham's young men. But always with one or several of her housemates—never alone. She avoided the attentions of the internes and staff doctors, preferring to obey the strict rules of the hospital which forbade anything remotely resembling friendship between male and female members of the staff. She was cool, efficient, but entirely impersonal with her male patients. The occasional one, who attempted to inject a sentimental note into their relationship and failing, ruefully came to acknowledge himself content, even grateful for her purely professional manner. She experienced a satisfying thrill of accomplishment in knowing herself to be a good nurse—efficient and trustworthy.

In Cranford, as in most hospitals, there existed a strong feeling of loyalty among the members of the nursing staff. Internes were the natural enemies of nurses and must be kept in check—with reservations. They were frank in their criticism of each other but they would fight tooth and nail at anything savoring of censure from an outsider or from the governing body. They would lie like gentlemen to protect one of their own and then lay down the law to that same one when all danger was safely past. Someone was always ready to smuggle a late culprit into the house and to cover any mistake she might make.

Judith found it much easier to adjust herself to conditions after she grew to know her fellow nurses and while there were some she did not like, especially, there were so many she did that she found it a simple matter to be pleasant to all. Thus she came to be regarded as "regular" and was admired by the entire staff. And she was happy—for the first time in her life. This was her life. She wanted nothing more.

She spent that first summer vacation at Mrs. Leeds' cottage on Lake Ontario where, at the insistence of her hostess and under the tutelage of one of her nurses, she learned to swim and to drive a car. It wasn't an especially happy vacation. Judith knew her friend was failing. She left her with a heavy heart. She felt that the unkind Fate

30

that had dogged her footsteps all her life was preparing to deal still another blow. She was tired and depressed when she deposited her suitcase in her room on the afternoon of her return. She chided herself with being a weakling, something no self-respecting nurse should own to. She tried to call up the determination to be self-reliant—hard, lifting her chin and glaring at her reflection in her mirror; but to no avail.

"You are a weakling, Judith Morley," she accused the sober face reflected in the glass. "You can't deny it. You have a bad heritage and what makes you think you can get anywhere—be anybody?" She beat her hands together and bit her lip in an effort to exorcise the little demon of despondency that possessed her.

To Isabelle, Brenda and the others who showed concern at her glumness she told something of Mrs. Leeds' condition, hoping they would accept the explanation as being the cause of her moodiness. And then she met the new interne—Doctor Lawrence Booth.

Larry Booth, fresh from a year at the Mayo Clinic, wanted special training under the chief—the locally famous Doctor Miles Cranford. With his advent things changed. Dark, handsome, clever—even brilliant, he set himself on that first meeting with Judith to break through the wall of reserve she had reared about herself and that had been so effective in discouraging unwelcome attention. She found it hard to resist this new man's friendly manner, his infectious laugh and his bold:

"Hello, beautiful! Now I know why I came to Cranford. How about a date?" These were his first words to her.

Instead of her usual cool squelching of the presuming male, Judith blushed and shook her head, too astonished to speak. She was glad when Isabelle approached.

"Fast work. Doctor!" Isabelle jeered as she joined them. "I bet Morley put you in your place. She's the gal who can do it."

"Sure she did," the young man replied. "My place is right beside her—all the way. Ever hear of love at first sight, Carey? It is Carey, isn't it? I'm rather good at names."

"Yes," Isabelle told him. "It's Carey and this is Judith Morley, just in case you don't know. Doctor Lawrence Booth, Judy. Interne extraordinary and menace plenipotentiary," she finished pertly. "Better give him the well-known brush-off, my child. He's not safe."

"Names don't amount to anything," the young man retorted unperturbed. "But I like your name, beautiful. Judith!" He lingered over the saying of it as if he found it pleasant. "It suits you, darling. Oh-oh!" he muttered as the chief hove in sight down the corridor. "S'long, gals. Be seeing you, gorgeous."

Isabelle laughed and departing shaking a warning head at the still speechless Judith. Doctor Cranford paused beside her for a moment, while down the corridor Miss Winters and the house physician hurried to overtake their chief. "Was that Doctor Booth? Where did he go? He's like a flea—here one minute and God-knows-where the next. Oh, there he is." He lifted his hand to summon the young man and Judith slipped away.

CHAPTER THREE

ALTHOUGH JUDITH gave young Doctor Booth no encouragement, he persistently followed up what he considered his advantage. He was so openly admiring, so stimulating in his banter that the little imp of fear in the back of her mind scurried away, and she found to her amazement that she could hold her own with him. She was nearer overcoming her innate shyness in his company than with any man she had ever met. Yet no sooner was she in bed and drifting off to sleep but that old feeling of apprehension would force its way through the haze of happiness that surrounded her and she would shudder and admonish herself that it was all just a pleasant dream. It mean absolutely nothing. Anyone as brilliantly attractive and popular as Larry Booth could never really fall in love with Judith Morley, Aunt Hepsie's great-grandniece and drudge. And there was the stain—the disgrace. No matter how unjust or even untrue it might seem, the fact remained there was a blot.

"You've come a long way, Judith Morley," she told the serious-eyed girl in the mirror on the snowy February night of her first stolen date with Doctor Booth. "And your polish looks bright and unmarred and real; but it isn't— not actually. Inside you're just a phoney—a drab little ignoramus—a scared kid with a doubtful background. Why, even my name may not belong to me," she whispered, her eyes enormous in her white face. "How do I know if it's mine? That's it. You put on a brave front but inside you're panicky—you always will be. You don't really believe Larry Booth means what he says—that he's falling in love with you—that he even hints of marriage. You know you don't. It's a line. He can't mean it—so soon. Anyway you can't let him. Better nip it in the bud—before he finds out."

In the five years Judith had been away, she had met no one from either Niles Corners or Medford. She hoped she never would. She realized she owed a great deal to

Doctor Wales who had vouched for her when she entered the training school at Procton. She had never gone back, but she felt sure Doctor Wales understood. She wrote him occasionally and he sent her a book now and then and once in a while a post card which she never was quite able to decipher. Every Christmas she was particular to include a gift for Mrs. Simpson in the box she mailed him and just as regularly the housekeeper included something for her in the box that came from the Doctor.

The Cranford Memorial Hospital was particular about its staff. The background of its thirty-odd nurses was supposed to be unimpeachable. There were times when Judith wondered at her being accepted so completely; but felt sure Mrs. Leeds' influence had a great deal to do with it together, perhaps, with her record as a student which she knew to be excellent. Her quiet reserved manner served to enhance the general opinion that she was well-bred—a lady. She smiled wryly at the thought and prayed she would never be found out.

Although she had doubts as to her real feeling toward Doctor Booth, she wanted to prolong the satisfaction his attentions gave her. And though she knew it couldn't last, she wanted to hold on to it just a little longer. She was hurting no one. She was arguing with herself in the manner habitual to her as she mounted the stairs to her room after depositing the candy and fruit on Williams' desk in the children's ward. She was late but it might do Larry good, if for a change she kept him waiting. It was usually she who waited. She thought of their last date when Larry had asserted that of course she would marry him when he got to be assistant surgeon. He had laughed as he made the statement and she had wondered which idea he had found amusing—her marriage to him or his appointment to the position as assistant to the chief. And with the old fear riding her she had laughed with him and retired into her shell giving him no encouragement if indeed he needed any.

She hadn't minded too much the kidding to which the

34

other girls subjected her. She knew and was grateful that they protected her from any possible discovery when she went out with him, so it came as a distinct shock on this occasion of her present date with Doctor Booth to learn that some of the older nurses didn't like him. She had heard her name mentioned as she passed the partly open door of one of the rooms in the nurses' home and paused for a moment, one hand against the door jamb, undecided whether or not to enter.

"Morley's a darned sight too good for him," she heard.

"It won't amount to anything. Don't worry. That guy's out for bigger game than a trained nurse—take it from me," another girl said.

"Just the same, someone's going to get hurt and it won't be the handsome Larry either." That was Owens, the special on the Towers hip case. What did she know about it? She had been in Cranford less than a month.

"Ye-ah," came surprisingly from quiet Beulah Scott. "It's just because Judy's so cool and—and—well—unattainable that she sort of challenges his ego. If she should actually fall for him and his line he'd give her the well-known brush-off pronto. It's a good sign the affair is still going strong. I gave hopes Judy'll take the initiative and give him the bum's rush."

There was a general laugh. If she wasn't so angry, Judith would have laughed with them. It was so unlike little Scottie to take any part in the general conversation. Well, it served her right for eavesdropping. But it wasn't true —or was it?"

"Just the same, Scottie's right," she heard one of the others say grimly. "He's absolutely ruthless. And demanding! Gosh! If there's one thing that burns me up it's the idea some internes have that nurses were made solely for the purpose of waiting on them. It's bad enough to have to cater to a full-fledged doctor; but when one of these smarty-pants starts giving me orders I feel like quitting my job. We have to be hypocrites and appear to find them perfect but it's darned hard work—sometimes. Booth's too

35

big for his britches." She gasped as she caught sight of Judith who had pushed open the door and entered. "I'm sorry," she said quickly. "But it happens to be the way your sweetie impresses me."

"Don't apologize to *me*, Hildreth," Judith said evenly trying to stifle her anger. How dare they criticize Larry? He was the cleverest man here even if he was so young and it wouldn't hurt any of them to serve him. He worked hard and they should all know it.

She felt the curious glances the girls turned on her and was uncomfortable. Well, she didn't care. Perhaps they were jealous of his attentions to her; but in her heart she didn't believe that to be true. She turned quickly and went on to her own room leaving a silence that was significant.

She dressed quickly, her anger giving her an added beauty. She left the house and walked quickly to the corner where she boarded a bus for downtown. Her heart quickened as she saw the green roadster Larry always borrowed parked across from the drugstore. He was inside having a drink at the soda fountain and she walked over to the opposite counter where she gave her order, ignoring the presence of the young doctor and wondering if he had seen her. If he had he gave no sign. He seemed deep in conversation with the man on the next stool and Judith lingered, looking over the piles of magazines.

Out of a corner of her eye she saw him consult his watch and leave his seat. There, he had seen her. He came over and they stood for a moment admiring one of the magazine covers. He held open the door and they left the store.

"Walk down to the corner, Judy," he advised her. "I'll pick you up there. That's Winters' nephew in case you didn't notice. If he blabs on us you'll sure be in the soup."

Judith stiffened. "Don't bother, Doctor Booth," she said coldly. "I'm not going with you. I'm taking a bus back to the hospital. You——"

"Don't be like that, darling," he whispered, lighting a

36

cigarette and flicking the match into the gutter. "It's you I'm thinking of. Be good to me, sweet—— He's staring out at us and I'm going back for more smokes. I'll be along directly."

He went into the store and Judith turned her steps back the way she had come. She would walk the mile and a half and maybe get rid of her anger, no longer against the girls at the hospital but against Larry Booth. How dared he? Yet she felt her wrath lessening with every step. After all, he was right. She couldn't risk the superintendent's disapproval. She walked on wondering if he was waiting for her at the corner. A horn sounded and a green roadster slid to a stop in front of her. He stepped out and stood close to her.

"Hop in, you nut," he ordered, grinning into her unsmiling face. "Don't be like that, precious. You know darned well what would happen if old Winters heard of this little jaunt. Come on, Judy, it's a swell night and— you're sweet," he whispered, close to her ear as he practically lifted her into the car and shut the door with a triumphant slam.

Rushing through the early spring twilight, her shoulder thrilling to the pressure of Larry's arm, Judith forgot the weariness of the day; forgot for a moment the feeling of dissatisfaction and regret that had persisted since her summary treatment of Rufus Grant and forgot her recent anger against her fellow nurses. It was all trivial. Larry was what she wanted just now. Tonight was everything that mattered. Her nerves quieted—her spirits soared.

"Did you know the chief has a granddaughter, Judy?" Larry asked suddenly and as Judith acknowledged that she didn't know it, he went on. "Neither did I, until this afternoon. She's been living in California with her mother but that lady has just taken unto herself another husband and Bernice has come on east for a long visit with her grandparents. The chief raved about her while we scrubbed after that messy emergency—you know, young Mendal, who crashed this noon. Oh, he'll live but I doubt if he'll ever fly again. I wish you had the case, Judy. I'm not sold on Clark—too maternal. What he needs is someone to arouse his interest—make him exert his will to live. I tried to get Carey after you were out of the question. Winters told me you're tied up with the Stacy brat for a solid week. Crazy! You couldn't kill that gal. But about this Bernice Cranford. The chief has invited me over for dinner tomorrow night. I'm highly flattered."

"You should be," Judith told him, stifling a twinge of jealousy. "The grapevine has it you're slated for the job of assistant surgeon in the fall. If you play your cards right——"

Larry took one hand from the wheel long enough to slap her smartly on the cheek nearest him. "Don't you dare insinuate that I make up to his granddaughter, Judy Morley. I'm out to get one girl and you know who she is, so don't try being coy with me." He was silent for a moment then turned to grin down at her.

Judith rubbed the slapped cheek with her gloved hand and gave an exaggerated whimpering "Ouch! That hurt, you big brute." But her heart threatened to suffocate her. He meant it. He really loved her!

"I intended it to," he replied. "Maybe some day I'll even beat you if I think you deserve it. You can be damned exasperating at times, you know." His voice dropped to the soft, slow, beguiling tones she found so fascinating. He patted her hand then pressed it until every fiber of her being tingled in response. "I'm mad about you, beautiful," he whispered. "There's no other girl in the world can oust you from the particular niche you occupy in this organ we call a heart."

After a moment he lifted his hand and reached into his pocket for cigarettes. He offered the packet to Judith who automatically took one and gave it to him. He slapped his pockets. "Got a match?" he asked.

Judith already had her bag open and lit the match. "Why doesn't Bill keep his car supplied with matches and smokes, Larry?" she asked as she had before. "What would you do if I wasn't here—prepared to serve you?"

His ready grin met her reproving glance. "Get another gal," he told her.

"And I believe that's just what you'd do," Judith said with a feeling of conviction. That was it. There were so many times when she was sure it was more than just liking she felt for him and then something would be said or done and the feeling vanished and she knew she was wise in withstanding his importunities. But he was such a darling she was afraid that some day in a moment of weakness she would let herself go. And would that be the best thing for either of them? Was it true what Scottie had said that if she said "yes" to his pleading he would lose interest, his ardor cool and he would turn to someone else? Oh, no— it couldn't be like that!

"You know better than that, Judith Morley," he said. "Why are you so skeptical? Why do you hold out on me? Why won't you give us both a chance? Why won't you let yourself be happy? Be yourself?"

Judith laughed ruefully. "That's what 310 asked me or rather ordered me to do this morning," she told him. "But it was for her own sake she asked it—not for mine. She had no particular interest in me except as a means to an end." That was it—a selfish request. Be yourself, not for your own benefit or pleasure or happiness; but to bring benefit, pleasure or happiness to the other. What did anyone know about another's self? How did he know but what you were being your true self at the moment?

"I bet you did what she wanted you to," Larry said. "That's why Winters put you on the Stacy case. What she needs is a personal maid and there was danger of another nurse quitting the brat cold after a few hours. Pretty kid, isn't she?"

"Very. It isn't the girl's fault she's a brat. She has been completely spoiled."

"I know. The parents are a pair of saps. They're old enough to be her grandparents. I bet she doesn't stay in the hospital the prescribed week. The chief was surprised she was submitted in the first place."

Judith smiled. "She had her reasons," she told him. "Girls always have their reasons for being docile—especially when it's out of character as in this case. She'll stay just as long as suits her purpose and not one minute longer. As it happens, her plan went haywire and she may leave before we know it. Still a week's hospitalization would do her good if she would rest and relax; but already she's rebelling at being deprived of visitors—the very thing her parents wanted her to be protected from."

"The sooner she gets out the better," Larry growled. "I have no patience with her sort. She should have been spanked soundly and often years ago——"

"Oh, for Heaven's sake!" she exclaimed. "A fine parent you'll make! Don't you know spanking is out of date? It tends to inhibit children. They should be allowed to develop their personailities—their hidden sources and tendencies without the slightest restriction."

"Bah!" Larry scoffed. "You don't believe that. I bet if Junior misbehaves you'll warm him good, only please don't threaten to tell his father when he comes home. I refuse to be held up as an ogre and feared by my offspring. I expect you to handle each misdemeanor as it arises."

Judith jeered. "Aren't you being a bit premature, Doctor Booth?" she asked. "Or is this purely hypothetical?"

"You're going to marry me, aren't you, Judy?" he asked as they found a parking place not far from the Ryder Hotel in Brampton. "I'm counting on it. You see, I made up my mind to marry a nurse—oh, ages ago, and the minute I saw you I knew my search was over. You just suit me."

Judith said nothing. Back in the remote niche of her mind the old doubt stirred. Now he pulled her hand through his arm and they stepped out briskly into the cool March night.

The hotel dining room was crowded. Judith was glad their table was near the end of the long room. She loved watching people. Almost the first person she saw was

Rufus Grant. He looked up and met her startled glance of recognition. He bowed formally and the girl seated next him leaned forward and said something to the other man in the foursome. Larry's eyes followed Judith's glance and the girl with Rufus Grant waved her hand to him. Larry stood up, then though better of it and sat down again.

"There's Liz Durnford, Judy," he said.

"I don't know her," Judith replied. "Should I?"

"You ought to. She's in the papers all the time. Fine horsewoman, flies her own plane, crack golfer and tennis player and an expert swimmer. I thought she was still in Florida."

Judith wondered if they had once been in love. He seemed a little flustered. He was extremely attractive and she saw the heads of girls turn in his direction from time to time, unconcealed admiration in their eyes. And yet she felt no particular pride in her present position. She had quickly grown accustomed to his appearing entirely unaware of other girls while he was with her. That was one of his charms, but tonight she had a feeling that beneath his apparent indifference he was definitely aware of the provocative glances cast his way.

She was annoyed at herself for being so critical. It had been a matter of pride with her that she was entirely devoid of jealousy. Why, she didn't know what it was. And yet she had resented Larry's evident interest and curiosity in his forthcoming dinner engagement to meet Bernice Cranford. If she was jealous, then she must be in love with him and of course she was quite sure it hadn't yet reached that point. She was determined it never should.

Rufus Grant and his friends left almost immediately and Liz Durnford drew him past the table at which Judith and Larry Booth were sitting. Introductions followed and Liz smiled warmly at Judith, chatting for a moment in a throaty contralto, before they moved on. Rufus Grant shook hands with Larry and met Judith's rather tentative glance with one of cool indifference. It was like a dash of cold water. She felt snubbed. It reminded her of Niles Corners days.

"So that's the great Rufus Grant!" Larry said as the two departed. "Big chap, isn't he? Rather fancies himself. How did you happen to know him, Judy?"

"Oh, he's the uncle of Angela Stacy's present heartbeat and came to see her at the hospital," she explained, her voice colorless.

"Well, one could see with half an eye he didn't make any particular hit with you, beautiful. I'm relieved. Say, this fish is good."

"So is mine," Judith agreed, glad to change the subject. But what did she expect? She had snubbed him first, hadn't she? If she had accepted his invitation to dine, she might have been going places with him right now instead of sitting opposite Larry Booth discussing the merits of the Ryder cuisine. She wondered where they were going. Maybe dancing or the movies. She and Larry were taking in a movie. Well, Rufus Grant was leaving town tomorrow and she wasn't likely to see him again. Again she experienced that feeling of dissatisfaction at the memory of her treatment of him but she banished it quickly. But if she had it to do over again——

In spite of the crowd they found seats in the theatre with little difficulty. It was several minutes before Judith recognized the man seated next her. It was Liz Durnford who brought him to her attention by leaning across Rufus Grant and saying:

"Hello! Do you mind if we change places, Miss Morley? I want to sit next to Larry. We have loads to talk about and I haven't seen him in ages. Rufe, you take my place and Miss Morley will move into yours. You're sweet," she smiled as the changes were made in silence.

Judith was annoyed but tried to make the best of it. Miss Durnford settled herself cozily and began at once a low-toned conversation with Larry Booth. Judith expected every moment to see angry heads turn and hear protests from those seated near them; but nothing like that occurred.

At that, she doubted if even Larry heard all that Liz whispered.

Rufus Grant sat tall and straight, his arms folded across his broad chest, his eyes on the screen. In the dimness Judith stole a glance at him and saw the grimness of his mouth and the coldness of his eye. A little laugh gurgled up in her. How perfectly silly! As she stared at him his brown eyes swerved in her direction but went quickly back to the screen again. The expression of his mouth never altered. Involuntarily Judith put out her hand and touched his arm.

"Are you real?" she whispered and immediately regretted the impulse for his hand caught hers and held it firmly and when she attempted to withdraw it she found she couldn't. Of all embarrassing situations! She looked at Larry and Miss Durnford to see if they noticed but at the moment they seemed absorbed in each other.

"Please!" she whispered and felt her cheeks hot.

"No," came the uncompromising reply.

Judith settled back with a sigh of resignation. It really wasn't disagreeable. His hand was warm and comfortable and she felt it was a good hand in spite of being a useless one. Under cover of the darkness her blushes receded. She wondered afterward what the picture was about. She saw very little of it although she kept her eyes on the screen. At its close, Miss Durnford turned to her with a little laugh of apology. Judith wrenched her hand free. It felt cold and lost in spite of her glove.

"Larry and I used to be great pals, Miss Morley," Liz explained. "You see, he used to visit next door to our place in Maine and we did a lot of things together. He tells me you're a nurse in Cranford Memorial where he is interning. I wanted to be a nurse once; but then there are so many things I want to do. Isn't life exciting, Miss Morley? I never seem to get enough of it." She shrugged into her mink coat and held out a small gloveless hand to Judith. "I hope we meet again, my dear. If you're a pal of Larry's I imagine we shall. Poor Rufus! Do you feel neglected?

I'm sorry. You two ought to know each other better," she said as they stood for a moment on the sidewalk before separating. "I bet you'd click. Good-bye—be seeing you before too long."

Beyond a quizzical glance straight into Judith's gray eyes, Rufus Grant had taken no part in the conversation. Larry hurried her along the crowded street to the place where he had left Bill's car. She was strangely excited. She could still feel the firm pressure of Rufus Grant's hand and blushed with annoyance. The night had turned cold.

"Liz is a great girl," Larry said as they sped along in the moonless darkness. "Rich as all get out yet as comfortable and easy as an old shoe. I wonder if she's engaged to this Grant chap. I wonder what he does for a living, if anything. All the Grants have money but I never happened to meet this one before. I'm sorry the evening was spoiled for you, Judy; but what could we do? There was one chance in ten thousand of our getting seats in the theater next to them—in fact, we were undecided whether or not we'd go to a movie—and yet there they sat. I hope you weren't bored, beautiful."

"Not at all," Judith replied, smiling wryly. "I like Miss Durnford. She's a real person, isn't she?"

The conversation was desultory after that. They were both tired and Judith wasn't long out of bed after Larry left her at the nurses' home. She was plagued by what had happened. Her conscience had troubled her ever since she so thoroughly snubbed Rufus Grant. She wished she had been a little less snooty. After all, perhaps it did seem absurd to make a fuss over a simple tonsillectomy when he had been led to believe it must be something really serious. She hoped he didn't know it was she who telephoned; but of course he must. Anyway, she needn't have followed instructions so literally. She could have given an inkling of the true situation. Yet why should she? Well, it was over and done with now and Mr. Rufus Grant was just a ship passing in the night—never to be seen again—she hoped. She examined the hand he had held so firmly. Not much like it was five years ago. No one would have wanted to hold that hand.

She wondered if he had a particular girl—if it was Liz Durnford and decided it couldn't be or she wouldn't have shoved him aside so summarily for Larry Booth. Her thoughts swung to the young doctor. There had been a subtle change in him after seeing Liz Durnford. Until then she had wondered how she could manage to keep cool in the face of his impetuous wooing. Now she puzzled over the question whether or not he and Liz had once been closer than mere pals. He had seemed to welcome the change that brought her nearer to him. Judith felt the girl's affection for him was obvious. Her heart sank.

"Don't be a sap, Judith Morley," she chided herself as she punched her pillow into a more comfortable position. "It can't possibly matter to you one way or the other. Use your head. Remember Aunt Hepsie and some of the unpalatable truths she drilled into you. Love is not for you. Love was the ruination of your mother and her mother before her. But I'm a Morley—I guess. Aunt Hepsie said I'm a Leeds—like my mother. I have a bad heritage. One can't get away from one's heritage."

She sad up in bed and raised one hand above her head. "I'll lay the Leeds ghost," she vowed, making a mental pledge. "I'll love and be loved. I'll be happy." But she said it miserably—without conviction—and lay down again burrowing beneath the blankets, her body writhing in an agony of rebellion until, from sheer exhaustion, she slept.

CHAPTER FOUR

JUDITH AWOKE to a feeling of depression. It was raining—a cold March drizzle. The curtains at her bedroom window swayed limply in the wind. Even the chirping of the first adventurous robin sounded melancholy. What ailed her? She stretched her arms high above her head and yawned widely. The alarm clock shrilled and she reached a hand to shut it off. Five-thirty. Already there were sounds of activity in the house; water running, a door shutting farther down the hall, suppressed laughter and the swishing of slippered feet scurrying along to the showers. She sat up and reached a groping foot for the mules she had slipped out of the night before. The morning was inky. She went to the window and stared into the blackness. The street light was reflected in puddles on the lawn. The leafless trees dripped mournfully and she felt the cold misty dampness against her face. She shut the window with a bang.

"What a day!" she muttered. "Well, it suits my mood." She grinned wryly as she recalled the events of the night before. "Don't be infantile, Judith Morley," she warned as she wrapped her robe about her slim body. "He isn't the first man to hold your hand during a movie and probably won't be the last—though I can't see what good it does them. It certainly gives me no pleasure—especially. If it seemed different this time it was just because he was no doubt trying to punish me for the snubbing I gave him. Or maybe he didn't consider it a punishment—rather a condescension—the stooping of King Cophetua so to speak."

She shook herself. "Snap out of it!" she ordered. "Remember Aunt Hepsie's advice to be hard—refuse to be patronized." After all, it was just an accident of birth that made Rufus Grant wealthy and Judith Morley poor. And in spite of everything, her sordid childhood and the disgrace that shadowed her life, she was responsible for none of it, and she would like Rufus Grant to know that she felt herself quite his equal. Her cheeks burned and she held her cold hands against them for a long moment. "Well," she told herself defiantly, "I snubbed him first. I'm glad he's gone—I hope he stays gone. Darn him!"

She felt somewhat better after that mild explosion and opened the door of her room to be immediately immersed in the life of the hospital. Nurses by twos and threes passed up and down the long, cold hall in all stages of dishabille. They greeted each other with more or less hilarity. Even the older nurses, who moved about more sedately, seemed pleasantly alive on this wet, gloomy morning.

"What's wrong with you, Judith?" Isabelle Carey wanted to know as Judith returned her greeting with a murmured, unsmiling "Good morning!" and went on to the showers. "Nightmare, or a sour note in the love-song?"

"Neither," Judith answered shortly. "I'm not troubled with either as you very well know."

"Don't feed me that, sweetheart," the other exclaimed imperturbably. She lowered her voice and murmured: "I saw you and Larry Booth beating it out Willow Road last night. Gee, but you've changed since that menace came here. Beware, darling! Winters'll get you if you don't watch out and who'll shoulder the blame? Not handsome Larry, I'll bet my last dollar. Maybe he's worth it; but I doubt it."

Judith said nothing for a moment. She was suddenly angry. What business was it of Isabelle Carey's? She bit her lip to refrain from speaking sharply. She never quarreled with her housemates although there were times when it was hard to keep her temper. She walked steadily on, Isabelle keeping pace with her.

"Yes," she said coolly. "I went to dinner and a movie with Doctor Booth last evening, Carey, and I don't care who knows it."

"Even Winters?"

"Even Winters with her silly rules. One would think this was a prison or a reform school the way she treats us."

"Listen, goon," the other soothed. "What's eating at your vitals? It isn't like you to indulge in morning grouches. Come on, tell Mama."

47

"Don't be absurd," Judith answered. "And you can broadcast the news of my infringement of rules if you like——"

"I don't deserve that nasty crack, Judith Morley," Isabelle told her aggrievedly.

"I'm sorry. Maybe it's the weather or perhaps I'm a little tired——"

"Not tired of nursing little Angelface, Morley!" someone exclaimed toweling herself briskly. "Gosh! We've all been envying you that job. A whole week with not a thing to do but help entertain Nottingham's Number One Oomph Gal. It's the only time in my experience that a tonsil patient has had such a fuss made over her. Is she really sick, Morley?"

Judith shook her head. "Not at all; but her parents think she will get more rest if she remains here than if she goes home even with a nurse accompanying her. I imagine she's had a pretty gay winter. Anyway, the family doctor has advised a week's hospitalization. Angela no doubt had her reasons for agreeing to it. She's spoiled but sort of sweet, too."

"Is she as pretty as they say she is?" another nurse asked curiously.

"Yes," Judith told them, glad to get away from personalities. "She's very pretty even without make-up. In fact, she's one of the few girls prettier without make-up; but of course you couldn't make her believe that."

She turned on the water full force to drown out further conversation. She wished the others would go on about their business. If they were finished in here why did they linger? But when, tingling and stimulated, she stepped from the shower a few minutes later, the girls were still arguing over their respective cases.

"I wish I could change jobs with you, Judy," Brenda Newton said as Judith joined them.

"Wh-at?" chorused the others.

"Well, I do," the girl insisted. "I don't think 270 knows I'm alive or at least that I'm not exactly hard on the eyes," she complained. "I hate this eternal acting so darned impersonal and businesslike. I like my patients to show a few human traits—occasionally."

"Faint heart and an inferiority complex never won a wealthy husband, Brenda," Isabelle reminded her. "Stick to it, old dear. When he gets better he'll notice your dimples and eyelashes and obligingly make a few passes at you."

"Shut up!" snapped Brenda with unaccustomed sharpness. "He's not that sort. Linus Porter is a gentleman, even if he is a grouch."

"Aha!" Isabelle grinned. "Methinks the gal really likes the lug, gall bladder and all. More power to you, darling!"

Judith patted Brenda's flushed cheek. "Don't let them bother you," she advised, feelingly.

Isabelle immediately turned on Judith, a wicked gleam in her green eyes. "And who might be the noble specimen holding you up in the Grade A corridor last evening, my fair lady? Two-timing the answer to a gal's prayer already! How do you do it, Morley? You'd make a fortune teaching charm, my friend. Ever consider it?" Judith prepared to pass the group. She had no desire to discuss Rufus Grant or Doctor Booth either. But Isabelle barred her way. "I saw him. A darned good-looking guy. I adore tall men. Did he give you all that stuff you had in your arms? Lucky you! Come on, tight-wad. Give! Who is he?"

"It just happens he was calling on Angela Stacy," Judith replied with dignity that was wasted on her tormenter.

"Wh-at?" jeered Isabelle. "That old man!"

"Old!" Judith exclaimed indignantly. "I doubt if he's thirty. Anyway, he's a friend of the family."

"Whose?" someone wanted to know, grinning.

"The Stacy family of course." Judith pulled off her rubber cap and shook her dark hair until it was a misty cloud about her face.

"What became of the spoils? Come on, gals, let's raid Morley's room. She's holding out on us." Isabelle pushed past Judith and started down the hall, the others following.

"I'm not either," Judith denied. "I took them over to Pediatrics. Angela didn't want them."

"Gosh, you're the darnedest!" Isabelle complained, turning back in disgust. "Couldn't you have given a thought to your starving neighbors? The kids get all the breaks in this joint."

Judith laughed mockingly. "You all look starved," she told them and went into her room, closing the door firmly behind her. Honestly, she thought, it was like living in an aquarium. There wasn't a particle of privacy. Sometimes she felt that even her innermost thoughts were public property. Isabelle Carey was the limit. Nothing escaped her sharp green eyes. Judith was fond of Isabelle although her insatiable curiosity often annoyed her. The girl knew more about the private lives of the patients in Cranford Memorial than the doctors did, or, Judith felt sure, even their most intimate friends. Sometimes she had a hunch Isabelle manufactured, out of whole cloth, many of the tales she told—they were so fantastic. But they made good entertainment when the girls gathered in one of the rooms to talk shop.

Isabelle knew the doctors, too; their goings and comings; their good points and imperfections; their hobbies and their indulgences, and had no illusions about any of them from the chief down. In fact, she ridiculed them all. Outwardly. she gave Miss Winters a great show of respect; but the girls all knew she loathed her. She imitiated everyone and held no one in awe. The girls were quite aware, even while they laughed and applauded when Isabelle mimicked an absentee, that just as soon as one of them left the room, she, too, would become the immediate object of her impersonation. However, it was quite useless to take offense and it was seldom that anyone did.

Isabelle was a law unto herself. Her patients adored her and she had the reputation of being a fine nurse. Judith had a sneaking suspicion the male members of the staff were a little afraid of her—of her sharp and clever tongue. At least, they seldom ragged her as they did the rest and neither did they go out of their way to help her in some tough or unpleasant spot as they did the others. But Isabelle didn't seem to mind. She went on about her business, rather cynical, often smart-alecky, but diligent and tireless. She had been nursing in Cranford Memorial for something like eight years and appeared to be perfectly happy. She was tall and chestnut-haired, carried herself with dignity—even hauteur, and was impressive in her uniform. Judith was always amused at the deference shown her by the doctors. She wished they could listen in on some of their get-togethers. She felt sure their opinion of Isabelle Carey would take a sudden nose-dive.

Brenda Newton was small and blonde with curly yellow hair, wide blue eyes, long thick golden lashes, dimples and in her nurse's uniform looked like a soubrette. Brenda, too, was a fine nurse. Patients enjoyed having her around. She was sunny, willing and capable.

She had been assigned to the Porter case in 270 for the reason that Linus Porter's mother had been a classmate of Brenda's Aunt Blanche when they were in Holyoke. Until Linus' gall bladder had gone on a rampage, however, Mrs. Porter hadn't recalled the friendship although Aunt Blanche had given her niece a letter of introduction to her old friend and had written Mrs. Porter to look Brenda up. When the lady insisted that Brenda be assigned to her son, she had no idea of the danger to which she was submitting him. Brenda had promptly fallen in love with the slender, grave young man and wondered why he appeared so completely indifferent to her charms.

Brenda was the hospital pet. Always sweet-tempered, docile and accommodating, the entire staff adored her. The internes vied with one another in doing her homage but she would have none of them. Surprisingly, she seemed to care little for men and in spite of her nursing experience and determination to treat all her male patients with reserve and complete lack of sentiment, she succumbed at once to the dark, rather taciturn young man in 270.

As Judith dressed she wondered about it. It was unfortunate if the affair had reached a serious stage, for she knew something of the Porter snobbery. Hadn't she been

Mr. Porter's nurse during a tonsillectomy? She didn't care for the Porters. Brenda was worthy of the best. Judith would like to point that out to the arrogant Mrs. Porter. But of course she wouldn't get to first base with her. She was surprised that Brenda was kept on the case, but it might just possibly be that Linus had something to say about it after all. Maybe he wasn't so indifferent as Brenda thought. Well, it would be interesting to watch.

It wasn't often a Cranford nurse fell in love with a patient although the reverse was universally true—only the patient usually recovered quickly after being discharged. It hadn't taken Judith long to realize that nursing was far from romantic. That it was hard work and long hours. That patients were more often cranky and unappreciative than not. That the staff was like any other group of people working together—good and bad—pleasant and disagreeable—those unselfishly eager to help and those who jealously refrained from doing one jot more than their allotted task. Judith felt the girls in her own particular group were the cream of the nursing staff. They had much in common. With the exception of Judith, their background was much the same and they seemed content with her story of being left an orphan when little more than a baby and living with an old aunt who had died just before she entered training school. They asked no questions and if Isabelle knew more, she kept it to herself. They argued and disagreed among themselves, but there was a loyalty to each other that defended them against the sly insinuations and intrigues of the rest of the staff. She hoped it wouldn't leak out about Brenda's lapse for it would mean a prompt reprimand from Winters and possible dismissal.

She wondered why she, herself, continued to take chances by going out with Doctor Booth. She was disgusted with herself. She promised it shouldn't happen again. This morning was one of those times when she had grave doubts of her true feeling for Larry. Could one truly love a man and be so critical—so in doubt? She gave an impatient sigh as

52

she pinned her cap in place and prepared to go down to breakfast.

"Forget it, Judith Morley," she told herself for the third time. "Keep your mooning until you're off duty. I'm coming," she called as a knock sounded on her closed door.

Brenda Newton was waiting outside. "I feel in my bones that something is going to happen today, Judy," the girl said as they followed the other nurses downstairs and along the gallery that connected the nurses' home with the main hospital building.

"You don't sound very optimistic," Judith commented. "Don't tell me you felt someone walking across your grave!" She said it lightly for she sensed the seriousness of the girl beside her.

"I don't feel optimistic. I have a hunch I'm going to be transferred to another case—that—— Oh, Judy, he's such a peach! I wish you could know him."

"But I thought he wasn't aware of your existence—that he——"

"I know I said so, but somehow I feel he—well— he likes having me take care of him although he doesn't say so. But his mother treats me like something to be endured against her better judgment. She doesn't approve of me, Judy".

"But I thought—didn't she ask for you, especially?"

"Yes; but that was before she ever saw me. I'm supposed to be a menace—blondes always are, the poor things." She shrugged slim shoulders as they entered the dining room. "What is to be will be, I suppose, and there's nothing I can do about it."

"Cheer up, Brenda," Judith counseled. "It may be only the weather. I'm pretty low myself this morning."

"You?" the other asked wonderingly. "I never saw you low before."

"Well," Judith advised grimly, "take a good look at me now, for I'm lower than a worm's vest button. I could bite nails and this is one morning when we're having oatmeal

53

and I loathe oatmeal." She drank her fruit juice and broke a piece of toast, buttering it slowly.

"Listen, Judy," Brenda said softly, watching the other warily. "If it's that Booth person who's got you down, don't let it worry you. He's a heel——Oh, I'm sorry," as Judith's face stiffened. "Anyway, I feel better for unburdening myself," she hurried on, pouring milk on her cereal. "If worse comes to worst, I can always go back home and work with old Doctor Mason."

"Don't be silly," Judith told her. "You are probably imagining the whole thing. Eat a good breakfast, my child. I mean to. We need it in the hard life we lead."

They ate silently for the rest of the meal although there was laughter and chatter all around them. Judith often thought it was a good thing Miss Winters didn't eat with them and that the supervisors were human. The superintendent would certainly get an eye-opener if she could hear some of the remarks made during meals. Her somber gaze swept the breakfast table and encountered Isabelle Carey's quizzical glance. She smiled mechanically and Isabelle made a wry face. The look had asked if all was now well with her and Judith's forced smile told her friend the dark mood still held.

Isabelle caught her arm as she prepared to mount the stairs to the next floor.

"You should have been at Chapel this morning, Judy," she said. "Her nibs was on the war path. Quote: 'There has been far too much shirking of one's religious obligations lately and it must stop. The staff is required'—not requested, mind you—'required to attend Chapel each morning unless illness or legitimate duties prevent,' unquote. Honestly, Judy, there was a mere handful present this morning. I got in late—just in time to hear the Wintry blast. It's sort of a shame, you know."

"I almost always attend," Judith told her.

"Not good enough, darling. Where were you at——"

"Oh, skip it, Carey," Judith said impatiently. "I'm getting sick of this place with its silly rules and——"

"Gosh, girl!" the other exclaimed. "You are in a bad way. Here's where I vamoose. See you sometime—after the weather clears."

"I'm sorry," Judith called after her.

Isabelle waved her hand and kept on her way down the corridor. Ashamed of her outburst, Judith slowly mounted the stairs. Aunt Hepsie used to say she could always tell when Judith had done something she shouldn't because it was then she showed temper, sulked and glowered at the world. Judith had come to believe that if she had one good trait it was her equable disposition. She was never hilarious and seldom grouchy; but this was one of the times when she wasn't proud of herself. Just why? As she slowly traversed the long corridor she reviewed the events of the night before for the second time. She was hurt and angry at the criticism she had heard and then what happened at the drugstore had added to the flame of her displeasure. It made a harmless case of breaking a silly rule something dishonorable—their meeting an illicit rendezvous.

She mentally shook herself. No use crying over spilled milk. She would tell Larry she woudn't go out with him again. With her mind made up, she felt better and opened the door at 310.

CHAPTER FIVE

MARIE HOOD's welcome was tinged with relief when Judith entered the Stacy room. Angela was asleep. The chart showed the patient had been restless and been given the sedative Doctor Branch had left for her. The two nurses stood for a moment looking down at the sleeping girl. How very lovely she was! Her long lashes lay dark against her sleep-flushed cheeks. Her bright hair was spread fanwise across the pillow and her fingers with the incongruous scarlet nails were relaxed on the white coverlet.

"Like an innocent baby," murmured Marie, cynically, "but I bet she could tell us a thing or two, and does she lead those besotted parents of hers a life! Wow!"

The girl stirred in her sleep and whimpered fretfully. Marie slipped out, one hand uplifted in a gesture of farewell, her mouth twisted in a grimace of distaste. Marie had little use for modern youth. She found it selfish and ungrateful. Give her a nice old party with pneumonia or a broken hip and she was happy. She felt repaid for all the hard work, the aching back and feet when her patient responded to her care and the chart showed an upward trend. But preserve her from teen-age youngsters, especially the wealthy ones they got at Cranford Memorial! Oh, well, Judith knew there were nurses and nurses, just as there were all sorts of patients. Some were grateful for everything done for them while others demanded more and more, never satisfied no matter how hard one tried to please.

"We have to take the good with the bad," she told herself beginning to feel better now that there was work to do. After all, this was her job and she loved it. She felt with each discharged patient a little thrill of pride for the part she had played in helping him back to health.

Angela slept until nearly nine when she demanded that all the flowers received the day before be brought in and arranged so that she could look at them without getting a crick in her neck. Judith made several trips to the small cool room in which the flowers were kept overnight and carried in baskets and vases, jars and urns filled with the choicest blooms Nottingham's florists could produce.

"Not bad," the girl pronounced them. "Now I'll have my bath and I'll wear the blue pajamas today and a fresh ribbon. Mother's going to bring a decent quilt for this bed. If I've got to stay here a week I can at least have things the way I want them. There's a bottle of my own particular perfume in my bag. I'll have just a drop on my hair ribbon. Then you may hand me my dressing-case. I'll take care of my make-up." She flushed as she caught the smile on Judith's lips. "What's so amusing?" she demanded.

"You take a lot of trouble to make yourself attractive, don't you?" she said. Then, impulsively: "And it really isn't at all necessary, you know. You're lovely just as you are."

Instead of being pleased at the sincerity of the other's admiration, Angela Stacy chose to ignore it. "Don't be servile, Miss Morley," she advised.

Judith's face flamed. "I assure you I am not in the least servile, Miss Stacy," she replied coolly. "Why should I be?"

"Oh, I don't know," the girl answered indifferently. "It really doesn't matter to me, only I detest people who fawn."

Judith gasped. "Why you little snip!" she said to herself, anger making her long to shake the impertinent chit before her. Instead she forced a smile and shrugged her shoulders which only served to annoy the patient.

"I'll have my toilet things right here on the bed after you've finished bathing me," the girl went on imperturbably. Her voice was thick and Judith said:

"I think you should not talk much today." She said it a bit grimly. "At least not until after Doctor Branch has been in."

"I shall do exactly as I please," Angela informed her pertly. "I'm all right. My throat isn't very sore. Tell the old fool to leave me alone. He gives me the creeps. I don't need him any longer. Anyway, why didn't Cranford come in last night instead of Twig?" She giggled at her own wit.

Judith wasn't amused. "We're paying him and his old hospital enough, Heaven knows."

"I suppose he felt there was no need. Doctor Cranford's time is valuable and he's a busy man," Judith explained.

"Oh, well, I don't care. But don't try to boss me just because I'm here and you're paid to be my day nurse. I put the other one—the night nurse—Hat—Bonnet—Hood—that's it—in her place."

"Don't talk nonsense," Judith said sharply and expected a rebuke but none came. Instead the girl stared at her with wide curious blue eyes in which lurked a spark of surprised admiration.

"You're rather pretty," she said wonderingly. "You've got nice hair and eyes." She appeared amazed at her discovery. Suddenly she smiled and perforce Judith smiled back. After all, this girl was little more than a child. "Why on earth do you stick to this job?" she went on. "I should hate it."

"Because I like it," Judith replied.

"But why? Is the pay good?"

"Fair."

The girl in the bed grinned knowingly. "I suppose there's always a chance of marrying one of your rich patients or maybe some doctor—they often marry their nurses, don't they? I suppose the chance is worth all the dirty work you have to do."

"There's not a chance in the world—well—scarcely a chance." Judith was annoyed. "Nurses rarely fall in love with their patients—rich or poor—and our associations with doctors are purely professional. We haven't time for romance here." While she spoke firmly, she felt like a hypocrite remembering Larry's ardent wooing of a few hours before. But it was none of this little brat's business.

She brought the desired dressing-case and turned away to busy herself about the room.

"Rufe's uncle was in to see me last night and was he cross!" came from the bed as its occupant applied lipstick and eye-shadow with a steady and experienced hand.

Judith was startled. She remained with her back to the bed while the girl went on:

"Personally, I don't see why he bothered to come just to see if I had heard from Rufe. It wasn't any of his concern. You should have been here, Miss Morley. He's terribly fascinating. All the women are mad about him. I could see that Hood fell hard for him but he never gave her a glance. It was a laugh. He might have noticed you, though. You're cute. I wish Rufe looked like him—tall and sort of masterful— I like red-headed men, anyway. But Rufe takes after his mother, although he gets his red hair from his father. I don't know where he got the million freckles— from some hick ancestor probably. Rufe's uncle's a farmer —believe it or not—a real, honest-to-gosh farmer."

Judith gasped again. A farmer! And she had snubbed him because she thought him a playboy—or was that the reason? She couldn't remember.

"Surprised you, didn't I? Well, it's a surprise to everyone these days. Why anyone should want to spend his life among the chickens and pigs is one for the book. Rufe and I get a big kick out of him. We ride him to a fare-you-well every time he comes to town. I was too sunk to do much razzing last night though. Anyway, I was the one who had the right to be cross—not him. I guess he saw it was no place for him—he didn't stay long."

Judith said nothing but went on with the job in hand. She didn't want to hear anything more about Rufus Grant. "Now if you're ready for breakfast," she said, "I'll have your tray brought up."

"Nothing but black coffee, please," the girl ordered. "I wish I could have a cigarette; but I promised the parents I'd refrain for two days. My throat ought to be well by tomorrow."

Mrs. Stacy entered while Angela was gulping her coffee. She wouldn't acknowledge that it still hurt her to drink, although Judith was sure that it did. Her mother hovered about the room, touching a flower here and there, and chattering about the weather and relating items of news she had gathered since she left her daughter the night before. Rufe had telephoned bright and early this morning. He was staying in camp the entire week as long as Angela was in the hospital. He was sending on the result of his first day's catch. Her father was pleased as could be. He adored fish.

"Listen," the girl abruptly interrupted the bright chatter of her mother. "I'm fed up with this place. I'm coming home—now."

"But—but—darling——" stammered her mother, looking pleadingly at Judith for help.

"That's for the doctor to say," Judith said levelly. Personally, she hoped the girl would leave. She was tired of being a glorified lady's maid and she was afraid if Angela continued to make insulting remarks about her and Hood, there would be something doing.

"Of course," Mrs. Stacy agreed, relief showing in her still pretty face. "If Doctor Cranford thinks it is all right for you to come home—maybe tomorrow, we shall be happy to have you; but darling, he agreed with Doctor Crowell that hospitalization was what you needed—a solid week of it without visitors. Don't you think you should stay the whole week, Angel?"

"No, I don't. I hate it here. I hate the hush-hushing that goes on all night even with my door closed. Last night I heard a woman scream 'He's dead!' right there across the hall." Judith had an idea she was putting on an act. She hadn't mentioned it before. "That Hood creature had the nerve to tell me I dreamed it. I didn't dream it, Mother. Somebody died in the room across the hall—I know it and I want to go home—now. I won't wait until tomorrow. Anyway, I feel as if I was buried—away from everything. I'm all right and I'm coming home." She swung her feet over the side of the bed and sat up just as Doctor Branch entered. Miss Winters followed and Larry Booth brought up the rear.

Judith wondered vaguely where Doctor Cranford might be and looked askance at the interne who was smiling at Angela and didn't meet her glance. The eyes of doctor and patient clung and Judith had the feeling they were conveying a message one to the other. At last Angela shrugged and turned away. Larry looked a little dashed. Doctor Branch prepared to examine the girl's throat and Angela made a face at him.

"She wants to come home, Doctor," her mother told him worriedly. "What do you think? She isn't happy here."

"Who is?" the resident asked curtly. "I'd say home was the place for her," he went on. "The hospital is for sick people. It isn't a hotel. By all means take her home. We can use this room.

Angela gasped. Her pretty face became scarlet with anger. "Just for that I'll stay," she said hoarsely. "We're paying for this room, and I shall stay as long as I choose and you just try to stop me."

Mrs. Stacy wrung her hands and murmured: "Oh, please, darling!"

Miss Winters looked properly sympathetic. It wouldn't do to antagonize the Stacys—they belonged to Nottingham's first families. "Perhaps, Doctor Branch," she offered placatingly. "the child is a little bored." Her glance, cold and accusing, settled briefly on Judith. "Maybe if she had a little jaunt into the solarium—just briefly, you——"

Doctor Branch made a noise in his throat. Angela transferred her glare of dislike to the superintendent.

"I'm not a child," she said coldly, "and I have no desire to visit your solarium even briefly. I'm going to stay right here until I decide to go home and then I shall go. This is my room and I'll thank you to get out and leave me alone."

Judith gasped again. Really this Angela Stacy was just about the limit. And yet she had a wild desire to laugh, too, at the expressions on the faces of the other occupants of the room.

Miss Winters stiffened then smiled knowingly at the embarrassed Mrs. Stacy. "I quite understand," she murmured commiseratingly. Angela turned her back. Doctor Branch got to his feet, his saturnine face breaking into a smile.

"I have no intention of trying to stop you, young lady," he said, stuffing the dangling ends of his stethoscope more firmly into the wide pocket of his white coat. "As you say, you have rented this room so by all means stay in it." He turned to the grinning interne who quickly sobered. "We'll drop over to Pediatrics next, Doctor. There may be real trouble over there. It would certainly be calamitous if we had an epidemic in this town right now, wouldn't it?" His slow, twisted smile swung to Judith and one eyelid drooped. He was spoofing. One could never be sure about Doctor Branch. The staff adored him but while he was an exceptional doctor he had no patience with either neurotics or fakes. He considered Angela Stacy and her kind a mixture of both.

He left the room followed by the superintendent and Larry Booth who had not given Judith so much as a glance. Of course that was all right. She really didn't expect him to notice her in the presence of Winters and Branch; but he needn't have been so completely oblivious of her proximity. She frowned in annoyance. Angela Stacy sat up in bed, her knees drawn up to her chin, and glared at her mother.

"This is absolutely the lousiest joint I was ever in," she muttered angrily. "Who does he think he is? Well, I'm getting out just the same. Get my clothes, Nurse. I'm going home. Epidemic! Let's go home before I catch something."

Angela Stacy left Cranford Memorial within the hour and Judith breathed a sigh of relief. Miss Winters called her into her office and demanded to know why the patient had been unhappy there. Judith could give her little enlightenment. The resident came in during the probing and dismissed the whole thing as nonsense—a spoiled brat's whim.

"Don't try constructing a mountain out of a molehill, Julia," he told the outraged superintendent bluntly. He knew she detested his using her first name in the presence of any of the staff, but he did it whenever he felt like teasing her. They had both been at Cranford for three decades and the years that had mellowed and humanized Doctor Branch had hardened and soured the superintendent until there was beginning to be talk of replacing her with a woman of less austerity.

"You forget yourself, Doctor," Miss Winters said frostily.

"Oh, come down off your high horse, Julia," the resident admonished chattily. "Dick Stacy isn't going to boycott this hospital just because his spoiled brat wants him to. In spite of his weakness in that quarter he's got money invested here and expects to get dividends. Cheer up, Julia, my girl. Nothing's as bad as you make it look. Anyway, I'm sure of one thing, Morley here isn't to blame."

"You may go, Morley," the superintendent said in her iciest voice and Judith murmured:

"Thank you, Miss Winters," and withdrew, but not before she heard the resident roar:

"Don't be a fool, Julia. You're cutting your own throat with your high-and-mightiness. Why don't you stand up for your nurses? They're a fine lot of girls. It's okay to let the patient think he's always right; but you don't have to let your nurses think they're forever in the wrong. They aren't —usually. I've told you that before."

Judith wished she might linger to hear the rest; but Doctor Cranford was coming down the corridor toward the superintendent's office. This was the night Larry was having dinner at the Cranfords' to meet the glamorous Bernice Cranford. She smiled dutifully in answer to the chief's greeting and went on to the elevator. Miss Winters said she was to go to the women's ward for the rest of the week. She didn't care. If it was supposed to be a punishment for her failure to keep Angela Stacy amused so she would remain the entire week in the hospital, she was glad she had failed. She much preferred something hard and demanding all her skill to acting as maid to the spoiled daughter of the Stacys.

CHAPTER SIX

JUDITH DIDN'T SEE Larry Booth to talk to for several days. It wasn't anything strange except that he didn't telephone either. It had been his custom to call her at least once a day or night just to hear her voice—he said. But since the Cranford dinner, she had heard nothing from him. She was a little piqued at his neglect wondering if he had found the chief's granddaughter as glamorous as gossip pronounced her.

Judith was still in the women's ward although the resident wanted her over in Pediatrics. Well, she didn't care where she worked; but she couldn't repress a feeling that Larry Booth was avoiding her. And then, one lovely spring morning, when doors and windows were wide to the sunshine and warm breeze, he got off the elevator just as she came along the corridor. She would have passed him with a mere "Good morning, Doctor," but he caught her hand.

"Here, wait a minute," he said. "I want to talk to you."

"Sorry," Judith murmured, drawing away. "I'm on duty. I can't stop to talk now."

He turned and matched his step to hers, his hand grasping her arm and slowing her progress. "How about a date tonight? I've got such a lot to tell you, Judy. How about going over to the New Brockway tonight—early?"

Scattering to the four winds went Judith's vows not to go out with him again. Her heart hammered in her breast— her spirits soared. She paused and turned her face to him, her eyes searching his. He met her gaze with one of bland comradery. She hesitated.

"I don't think so," she said, trying to keep the excitement out of her voice. "Anyway, I've used up all my late time——"

"Borrow from someone—Carey—Newton—one of them will swap with you. I've got to talk, Judy. Oh, come on—be a sport and let's go. Things are shaping up my way and —— But I'll tell you tonight."

"All right," she agreed. "I'll see if I can change with someone. Call me later."

"I'll give you a buzz after dinner. Good girl!' he commended and swung her hand, letting it drop as Doctor Branch came into the corridor from one of the semi-private rooms and called to him.

Elation and doubt fought for supremacy in Judith's thoughts. He seemed almost like his old self—eager for a date. She had been silly to think he could change so quickly. She knew Isabelle had a date for tonight but wasn't sure about Brenda. Maybe Brenda wouldn't want to change. If she didn't—well, then she would know it wouldn't be right for her to accept Larry's invitation. Crazy! Brenda had to be willing, that's all; for Judith knew she must keep this date with Larry if she never had another. She wondered why she felt as she did—that somehow tonight would be the last time she would go out with him. Brenda had to change with her. Brenda was willing.

It was a long day, unseasonably warm, and Judith thought it would never end. At that, she was delayed, the night nurse failing to relieve her on time. She was nervous and annoyed. It would happen on this one night when she wanted extra time for dressing. At last she was free and hurried down the corridor to the elevator. It was nearly seven-thirty. She wondered if Larry had already called— he usually called about half-past seven if they were going out. The elevator dropped to the ground floor. She ran along the gallery and up the stairs to her room. She wouldn't go down to dinner. They would no doubt eat some place on the way if Larry hadn't eaten. Anyway, if she was dressed in time she might stop in at the diet kitchen for a glass of milk and a cookie. Her hands shook as she brushed her hair and she forced herself to calmness. Larry had said Johnny Drake's Bluebonnets were to provide the music and the night promised to be gorgeous—a full moon and mild as summer. She opened her closet door for a glimpse of the new frock hanging there.

There was a knock on her door. She was wanted on the

telephone. She caught up a robe and followed the maid downstairs. Larry's voice sounded queer. He was terribly sorry but he couldn't make it. He was tied up and couldn't get away. There was a faltering uncertainly about his apology. It didn't ring true. Perhaps she was altogether too suspicious. Maybe she was jealous. She hadn't seen him since that dinner date at the chief's house. Perhaps——

"Don't be an idiot, Judith Morley," she told herself sharply as she slowly replaced the telephone in its cradle. But she knew with a sick feeling in her heart that this was the end. Things would never again be the same between her and Larry Booth.

Back in her room, she took down the new maize dancing frock and held it against her body. It was very becoming. Someone knocked and she called "Come," and turned to hang the gown on its padded hanger.

Isabelle Carey entered, a robe held tightly around her hips. "O-oh!" she exclaimed. "Lovely! New?"

Judith nodded, her hands caressing the soft folds of satin.

"Going out?" the other asked, her eyes on the dancing pumps Judith wore.

"No," the girl replied. "Just admiring my new outfit." She held it against her for her friend to see. "I sort of like it," she confessed.

"Uh-uh," Isabelle murmured. "I wish you'd pinch-hit for me tonight. Will you? I'm about dead." She looked it.

"Pinch-hit? What doing?" Judith asked warily.

"I have a date with Dick Wilson for the Club party. I didn't want to go in the first place. He's getting to be a pain in the neck since he got his pilot's license. Can't talk of another thing. Anyway, I want to hear that lecture Carter's giving at the Center." Judith eyed the other girl until she changed color and her head lifted defiantly. "Well?" she asked. "How about it? Will you or won't Larry allow it?"

"You make me sick!" Judith said sharply. "Larry Booth

has nothing to say about what I do and don't do, and you know it."

"I don't," Isabelle said mildly. "Will you help me out?"

"So it's Carter now, is it?" Judith inquired still coldly.

"Does that mean you won't be a pal and do it?" Isabelle's voice was aggrieved. "I'd do it for you—with anyone but Doc."

Judith still hesitated. "Why not?" she asked herself. A vision of Larry Booth and the lovely blond Bernice Cranford, perhaps dancing together or riding along the country lanes on this perfect night, made her snatch the dress from its hanger. "I'll go," she said, "if Dick won't mind the switch."

Isabelle laughed. "Don't worry. You'll be someone new —a fresh ear to listen to his rhapsodies. Thanks, Judy. I'll do something for you one of these days." She turned to leave the room. "Want me to explain to Dick or will you?"

"I'll explain," Judith told her. "No need for you to perjure your soul. I feel like dancing and you don't and he can rave to his heart's content—I needn't listen if he bores me. Dick and I understand each other. Run along and listen to Carter—I hope he appreciates your being there. Don't expect too much, though. Doctors are an unappreciative lot."

"You should know," Isabelle murmured and closed the door softly behind her.

If Judith heard she made no sign. She caught up her wrap and went downstairs. Dick Wilson was coming in the front door as she reached the lowest step. He came to meet her.

"Hi, Judy!" he greeted her. "How you fill the eye! Isabelle ready? Where you going?"

"With you."

"Swell!" the young man enthused. "How long will Isabelle be? What's she doing?"

"That's it. She isn't going with us. She finds she must attend a lecture over at the Center and asked me to pinch-hit for her. Do you mind—too much?"

"Mind?" he asked. "You know darned well I'm thrilled to get a date with you. Doc's been riding herd on you so close this past winter no one else can get a chance. Come on, let's go."

It was as easy as that. Judith thought it would be. Dick Wilson was the most adaptable man she had ever known. While he was to all appearances devoted to Isabelle Carey. he was equally willing to date any substitute she might provide if at the last moment she wanted to do something else. Judith wondered what he would have done if Isabelle couldn't have found a substitute and had refused to keep her date with him. Probably he would have gone stag and had a very good time just the same. He was that sort.

Judith was scarcely seated in the car when he began on his favorite topic of conversation. It wasn't far to the Club and he had but nicely started on his subject when they turned into the wide brightly lighted entrance of Nottingham Country Club. Dick was all for sitting out for a while but Judith was eager to go inside. She didn't blame Isabelle for being bored. Dick's ravings were those of a small boy with his first kite. She wondered what he intended doing now that he had a pilot's license. He had already wrecked two planes and it was a wonder to everyone who knew him that he had gone on to get a license. But, as Judith thought grimly, money can buy anything. He had enlisted but been turned down because of a slight lameness, the result of infantile paralysis in his childhood. Now at twenty-nine he looked hale and hearty enough for anything but he was debarred from the army, the navy and the air force. Dick didn't seem to mind much. He said he would fly anyway, and apparently he was right.

Judith was hungry. She had forgotten her intention to stop in the diet kitchen. She had eaten nothing since lunch and hoped Dick would suggest dinner. He didn't, but two of his friends were on their way to the dining bar and suggested they make a foursome. It was okay with Dick who immediately became oratorical about his new plane. Bill Towne listened avidly and a bit enviously to the recital while Mrs. Towne looked at Judith with raised eyebrows that later turned into a frown of displeasure.

"Can't you choke him off?" she asked through clenched teeth. "Bill's crazy for a plane and I refuse to consent to his having one. I detest the things and—well—I don't want my child to lack a father when he makes his appearance next fall. He'd go up and up and forget to come down until something gave out and he crashed." She shuddered. "Darn that Dick Wilson!"

Judith wondered how it was that Bill wasn't in the army. She said: "Does he want aviation?"

"Oh, he's on the deferred list and now that he's over age he won't go at all; but he's mad about flying. The baby's coming has given me a respite—but——"

"He looks as if he knew his own mind," Judith ventured.

"That's just it. I get sort of sick every time he mentions it so he hasn't referred to it lately. Now Dick has started it all over again. I wish we hadn't come." The girl's eyes were tortured and she fidgeted with her glass, turning it round and round until Judith had a strong desire to snatch it away from her.

"Oh, he probably hasn't any idea of doing anything about it right now," Judith soothed. "And if he sits and listens much longer to Dick's maudlin ravings, I doubt if he'll want to—ever. Listen."

They listened and heard Bill try to get a word in now and then without much success. His "Well, now," and "I think" or "But, listen," had no effect on the continuous flow of detail issuing from Dick's excited lips. Mrs. Towne giggled.

"I see what you mean," she said and nodded to Judith. She relaxed and finished her ginger ale, wrinkling her nose childishly. "It always prickles," she explained.

At last Bill caught his wife's eye and suggested they dance inasmuch as that is what they came to the Club for. Dick wasn't finished but Judith laid a determined hand on his arm.

69

"Come on, Dicky," she murmured placatingly as she saw his disappointment at Bill Towne's desertion. "I have to leave rather early, you know, and I want to dance."

"Okay," he agreed, the frown exaporating.

The first persons Judith saw when she entered the huge ballroom of the swanky Country Club were Rufus Grant and Liz Durnford. Liz waved a hand at her and said something to her partner who promptly swung her over to the corner where Judith and Dick were standing.

"Hello, Dick!" Liz greeted Judith's escort. "So at long last you have your license?"

"Oh, it hasn't been as long as all that," Dick protested. "Hi ya, Grant?"

From Rufus Grant's expression, Judith surmised that Dick's plane was an old story. But it was Liz Durnford's line to be interested in everyone's pet hobby. Judith wondered if that was the reason for her popularity. Certainly she wasn't at all beautiful. But she had a charming manner and friendly smile that made one forget her too large nose and mouth, her somewhat leathery skin and straight, mouse-color hair. Judith was sure she could improve her appearance if she desired. The gown she had on right now was not a bit becoming. And her hair—surely something could be done with her hair. She thought of all that Mrs. Leeds had done for her, and Judith wondered why someone didn't take Liz in hand. Perhaps with her money and social position she felt it wasn't necessary. That must be it. But to Judith it seemed rather a shame, for she liked Liz Durnford. Now she turned to Judith and asked:

"Where's Larry? He told me he would be here tonight."

"A doctor is never quit free." Judith explained. But it was to the New Brockway in Waverly Larry had invited her. He wouldn't dare take her to the Country Club lest they run across some member of the Cranford Board or the chief himself. Not that Doctor Cranford went in much for dancing; but he liked to be with the townspeople. He was a definite social success.

"No doubt that's why Judy's with me," Dick added. "His

loss is my gain. My date stood me up—too. We're sort of consoling each other—Judy and I. Right?"

Judith said nothing but she wondered how Dick knew Larry had let her down, or was it just a guess? She felt Rufus Grant's brown eyes on her.

"Why, there's Larry now. Who's that with him?" It was Liz who spoke and she turned quickly to slip her hand through Judith's arm. But Judith had glimpsed Doctor Booth enter with the most beautiful girl she had ever seen. It must be Bernice Cranford. So that's why he had broken his date with her.

"Let's dance," Dick suggested with unaccustomed tact. Judith was grateful. She was sure Larry had seen her for, as the evening advanced, he appeared to avoid her. Later, when Rufus Grant suggested they get out for some air, she welcomed the idea.

"Will you be warm enough?" he asked solicitously as they stepped out upon the wide balcony that extended along two sides of the building. "Wait, I'll get you a wrap and then let's go down and along the terrace to the pool. It's a swell night."

"Grand!" Judith replied, with a show of enthusiasm she was far from feeling. Larry had lied to her. At least he had led her to believe he was on duty tonight. And just a few nights ago he had asked, no, he had told her she must marry him. Her nails bit into the palms of her hands. What a fool she had been to put reliance in any man. She had been warned. There was no excuse for her. She was just as weak as the rest of the Leeds women. Her head lifted proudly. Well, at least she hadn't gone the whole way. Suppose she had accepted him. Suppose she had become openly engaged to him. She closed her eyes and lifted her face to the soft spring breeze. Something like a prayer of gratitude went up from her heart that she had been spared that—at least.

Rufus Grant was back almost at once with a wrap, whose, Judith didn't know or care. He placed it about her shoulders and they went down the wide stairs to the terrace below, passing a few couples who were far too interested in their own affairs to notice them.

The night was thick with stars, the full moon shedding a soft silvery light over a world pulsing with the return of spring. Judith felt it even while her heart was torn with anger and hurt. How could Larry do this to her? This man beside her, walking silently, his hand warm and gentle on her elbow, knew that she as well as Dick Wilson had been "stood up." Instinctively, she pulled away from the guiding hand only to stumble blindly.

"Careful," Rufus cautioned softly, putting out a restraining hand. "Sort of rough right here. We'll soon be on level ground and then you can be as independent as you like."

Judith said nothing for a moment, then grimly pulled herself together. What did it matter anyway? If Larry was that kind she was well rid of him. What an idiot she was! All winter she had been telling herself that she couldn't possibly care for Doctor Booth and that she was sure his attentions meant absolutely nothing serious and now when she was proved right in her assumption, she was angry and hurt. She had no right to be. She had known from the first that such happiness could not be hers—that love was not for her. She had deliberately played with fire and now she was crying because she had been burned. A weakling. No She would not be. She laughed mirthlessly.

"I have to be independent, Mr. Grant," she said.

"No one is independent," he disputed firmly. "Each of us is dependent on his fellows whether he acknowledges it or not."

"Of course," Judith agreed impatiently. "I was referring to a different sort of independence—that of the spirit."

"Even there we are not entirely independent," he asserted. "No one is free, you know."

"Oh, I don't feel like arguing tonight, Mr. Grant," Judith retorted. "It's—it's too wonderful out here——"

"Couldn't you manage 'Rufus'?" he asked tentatively.

"Why?"

"Oh, it's—well, it's friendlier," he explained.

"But—but——"

"Or don't you want to be friendly?"

"How can we be friends?" Judith asked, interested in spite of herself.

"By just being friendly. If you would shed that impersonal cloak you wrap so closely about your really charming self and give a chap a chance, we could have a lot of fun together—that is—unless——"

"Well?" Judith asked, stiffening involuntarily. Would he dare mention Larry Booth?

"Of course I don't want to trespass—if you're tied up with someone—Doctor Booth—but I don't believe you are. Perhaps it is wishful thinking on my part but somehow I—well——" He stammered the last and Judith suddenly felt like laughing although there was nothing in the least humorous in the situation.

"I'm not tied up with anyone—except the hospital, Mr. —Rufus," she told him. "I'm free, white and twenty-three. Doctor Booth and I have been good friends—are yet for all I know. That's absolutely all." She drew a long breath and unconsciously quickened her pace.

He matched his step to hers. "You sound somewhat doubtful. Has something happened? I'm sorry I sound like an inquisitive busybody."

"You do," Judith said coldly. "Doctor Booth and I work in the same place—see each other every day—nearly. Just because he saw fit to break a date with me tonight it—well —it doesn't constitute a crime, you know."

"I disagree with you, Judy," Rufus said earnestly. "And wasn't it you who assured me you never broke your engagements?"

"What a long memory you have, my dear—Rufus!" Judith said ironically.

The better to convince you of your desirability, my dear— Judith," he countered. "Come," he wheedled. "Toss the chip off your shoulder and let's be friends. What say?"

"Is friendship so easily established?" she asked.

"In this case, yes."

"What makes you think so? I doubt if we can be friends," she said seriously. "We have so little in common."

"How do you know?"

"Oh, we belong to different worlds——"

"Don't be a snob, my dear girl. You mean you work for a living? Well, so do I——"

Judith laughed. "Work? Our ideas of what constitutes work differ."

"Don't talk nonsense," he said sharply. "I assure you I work hard. What does it matter if I have a few dollars laid away, left me by my father? The fact remains that I work with my hands and with my brain and heart. I love my work and what's more I do a good job. From what I hear, you do the same. Tell me wherein the difference lies?"

"Oh, what does it matter? There's a vast difference but —maybe you wouldn't understand."

"No. Work is work and if it is done conscientiously and well, it is commendable and the laborer worthy. Who was it said: 'Who sweeps a room as by God's law makes that and the action fine'?" He laughed a bit self-consciously and Judith liked him better. "I sound like an exhorter. I didn't mean to preach," he muttered apologetically.

"Oh, that's all right," Judith assured him. "I feel properly rebuked."

"And you are willing to be friends?"

"For as long as you like," she agreed demurely. She had forgotten her anger at Larry's partial lie.

"And just what does that mean?" he asked quickly. "Just what do you think friendship is?"

"It is something fine and splendid," the girl said seriously. "Something that precludes doubt; that obviates the necessity of explanation of one's actions; that is long-suffering and kind——"

"You're confusing it with love, Judy," Rufus chided. "Mere friendship can't be all that."

"Can't it? True friendship can. So, maybe we'd better just leave our relationship as is——"

"I still hold out for friendship—no matter what your definition may be. Friendship—I'm all for friendship and I love your description of it. Let's be friends, Judy—long-suffering and kind. I'll be the first if you'll be the second. How about it? Is it a deal?"

He held out his hand and Judith put hers into it. They shook solemnly.

"Say, what is this?" demanded Dick Wilson falling into step beside Judith. "Here I am calmly stood up for the second time in one short evening. It's too much. There ain't no justice in this world any more. Come along, Judy. Time's a-wastin' and I bet Liz is ready to murder you, Rufe."

"Oh, no, she isn't," Rufus said complacently. "She's much too self-sufficient and popular to have to depend on me or any man."

"She's grand!" Judith said enthusiastically. "I think I like her as well as any girl I ever met."

"Everyone likes Liz," Rufus agreed. "She's a swell girl."

"The only thing is she knows too darned much," Dick complained. "Offered to take me up in her plane and give me a few pointers. Ha!" he exploded. "That's the woman of it. Just because she's had a few more hours in the air and had her license a couple of years. Makes me sick. Anyway, I like my women less—more—well, womanly—feminine. I don't care for these independent, athletic gals."

Rufus laughed, and pressed Judith's arm.

"Is that why you like Isabelle?" she asked, demurely.

"Well, nursing's a womanly job, isn't it?" he demanded.

"Of course it is," Judith soothed, patting his arm. "And Isabelle is a wonderful nurse—lovely, too."

"I'll say she is," Dick agreed. "I'm nuts about her."

"But aren't nurses pretty independent, Dick?" Rufus asked.

"Not the right sort," the other asserted, positively. "They have to put on an act, of course; but come right down to it they're the sweetest, kindest, most sympathetic creatures in the world."

Rufus shouted with mirth. Judith laughed ruefully. "What a picture you paint of my profession, Dick," she said.

"O'oh," he murmured as they neared the brightly lighted clubhouse. "I forgot you're a nurse. Well, that's the way I find 'em. Maybe some nurses are sour and cranky but *my* nurse isn't."

"Of course she isn't," Judith said and recalled Isabelle's gamin antics when she was mimicking her superior for the benefit of her housemates. "Isabelle's a darling."

It was much later that evening when Judith saw Rufus Grant again. He was dancing with Bernice Cranford and grinned as he caught Judith's eye. When the dance ended she found Larry Booth at her shoulder.

"Don't think me a heel, Judy," he begged, his blue eyes shamed. "I couldn't get out of it."

"That's all right," Judith told him coolly. "I'm having a marvelous time."

"Who did you come with——" he began when Bernice Cranford and her escort came up to them. Judith's lip curled as she saw Larry's uneasiness. Rufus introduced the two girls and Judith felt the other's antagonism.

"So you work for Gramp?" Bernice said, her gentian eyes raking the other from the top of her dark head to the hem of her flaring maize skirt and gay, dancing shoes.

"And so happy about it!" Judith replied sweetly.

"Gramp's a lamb," Bernice agreed. "But isn't hospital work frightfully hard and—and disagreeable?"

Judith laughed. "Ask Doctor Booth. Without doubt I'm prejudiced."

She felt rather than saw Rufus Grant's grin of approval. "Dance, Judy?" he asked and the other two stared as they drifted off.

"Beautiful, isn't she?" Rufus said as they reached the farther side of the huge room.

"As a dream," Judith said without venom.

"She looks like a girl who would get what she wants from life," Rufus went on.

"No doubt about it," Judith agreed once more.

The man laughed and drew her a bit closer. "You're not usually so amenable. Is the serum working so soon?"

Judith raised long-lashed gray eyes to his and he caught his breath at the look in them. Dark, stormy with deep hurt, they told him more than he had dreamed. She did care for this good-looking Larry Booth, then. The feeling was something more than friendship.

"I'm sorry, Judy," he whispered.

Judith bit her lip. "Don't be," she said sharply. "I—I don't know why you should be."

"How about tomorrow night?" he asked hastily. "How about a trip over to the New Brockway? They have a splendid orchestra over there this week."

"You forget I'm a working girl, Mr. Grant," Judith reminded him, trying to make her tone light. "I don't get another late night until after the first. That's more than a week off. I've used up all my privileges for this entire month. As it is, I owe for tonight."

"Well, I make a bid for the first evening you have, or do you get time off during the day?"

"Oh, I get an afternoon a week off when I'm on day duty; but you're supposed to be busy too, or were you spoofing?"

"No, indeed. But I, too, get an afternoon off occasionally. Perhaps I could make mine the same afternoon as yours. How about it?"

"It might be arranged," she said almost indifferently. She was suddenly very tired. She wanted the quiet of her own room, free from the kindly but, she felt, prying eyes of this tall, good-looking young man. "It's getting late, Rufus. Find Dick for me, will you? I must get back to the hospital."

"Okay," the young man murmured, expertly steering her through the maze of dancers to the opposite side of the room where he had spotted Dick Wilson's fair head above the blond one of Bernice Cranford. Judith motioned to Dick just as the music stopped. The two came over to where she and Rufus stood. Larry Booth hurried up to join them.

"Let's go," Judith whispered to Dick who promptly said goodnight to the others and followed her into the hall. "I'm sorry if you're not ready to go, Dick," she explained; "but I've really got to get back."

"Okay by me," he returned agreeably. "It's sort of lousy anyway. Beautiful and icy—that's the Cranford female," was his pronouncement. "Who does she thing she is, anyway? Garbo or something?"

"I wouldn't know," Judith replied. "I won't be a second," she promised as she left him to get her wrap.

She was beautiful, Judith conceded that much; but she didn't like her—not one bit. She wondered just why she should be enamored of Larry Booth. He wasn't too well off. Of course he was handsome but there were any number of better looking men right there in the room with her— wealthier, too. Perhaps it was his prospects of becoming her grandfather's assistant that intrigued her. The chief could do a great deal for him—probably more if he were his grandson-in-law.

Judith ignored the other girl's in the powder room, not even glancing at a mirror, but caught up her wrap and left. She thought interested glances followed her but decided she imagined it. After all, she knew practically no one there.

CHAPTER SEVEN

A WEEK LATER, Judith was assigned to night duty in the same ward in which she had been working days. She hadn't had much night duty this spring and supposed she was in for it. Work in the women's ward at Cranford Memorial was considered the toughest in the entire hospital. The semi-private rooms weren't so bad; but the long open ward of some twenty beds was always filled to capacity and the nurses declared Cranford got the town's noisiest women available. It wasn't to be wondered at for the beds were all free, the gift of Mrs. MacOmber, Nottingham's wealthiest woman, as a memorial to her mother. The staff had the idea that being put in charge of the Charity Ward was a case of being sent to Coventry and yet Judith rather enjoyed taking care of these noisy, rebellious and often ignorant women. It was sort of like going back a decade to the time when Aunt Hepsie was ill. The complaints and demands of the patients here had a familiar sound. Judith felt she had served her apprenticeship in the cottage in Niles Corners. This was graduate work.

She hadn't seen anything of Rufus Grant since the night of the Country Club dance and very little—mere glimpses —of Doctor Booth. She tried to convince herself she was relieved; but there was a feeling of loss in her heart that all her devotion to duty seemed not to dispel. It was her second night in the ward and at long last the occupants of the twenty beds were sleeping. What a night it had been! Mrs. Luini had been brought in at a little after midnight together with two others from the midst of a free-for-all in her restaurant. The two with her were comparatively quiet after their cuts and bruises had been taken care of, but while Mrs. Luini's injuries were superficial, she continued groaning and moaning and calling down maledictions on everyone. She had been examined in Receiving, found to be suffering from hysteria following a fit of some sort brought on by the raid, and was sent up to the ward. Judith had tried in vain to make her comfortable. Her Giovanni was in jail together with three other men and it wasn't right. Her man was innocent as an unborn bambino. She clenched her fists and cursed the police, the doctors and the nurses who tried to quiet her.

Judith came to wish the police had taken her along with her Giovanni. She refused a sedative on the score they were trying to poison her. She knew she was dying and demanded a priest and her Giovanni. When Judith assured her there was really nothing serious the matter with her if she would only calm down and relax, the woman promptly had hystetrics again. The other patients glared at her and complained they couldn't sleep. Only her two friends were quiet. They appeared completely indifferent to what was going on. Mrs. Luini was a huge woman—weighing well over two hundred, tall and muscular. She shoved the nurses aside as if they were infants, continuing to complain and wail at the injustice shown her Giovanni.

At her wit's end, Judith sent for the resident. It was well after two and the ward was in an uproar. Why had this woman been sent here anyway? She had rallied in Receiving and been quiet while the doctors were present. It wasn't until she was put to bed in the ward that the trouble began. She might better have been sent home.

"Rallied!" Judith grinned at her fellow nurse. "She's a super-woman. Look at those arms, Ingham. Let Branch handle her."

But is wasn't the resident who answered the summons. Larry Booth strode into the ward and Judith's heart did a flip-flop. In spite of his hospital white he looked disheveled and he certainly was cross.

"What's up?" he demanded. "Here, you! Stop that noise!" he ordered sharply of Mrs. Luini, who immediately pulled out the fortissimo stop and held it.

Judith couldn't repress a grin although she was heartily sick of the woman. Little Amy Ingham didn't quite suppress a giggle. Larry glared at them both then turned to Mrs. Luini.

"What's the matter with you?" he demanded. "Are you in pain?"

"Pain, he asks," the woman roared. "I'm one big pain. My head hurts. My back hurts. My heart hurts and these girls—these nurses they call themselves in their slick white dresses—they just shush me—they don't do nothing. My Giovanni——"

"I know, I know," Larry soothed, going immediately into his already famous bedside manner, "but we have to put up with them, don't we?"

Judith gasped and Amy scuttled over to the bed in the farthest corner where she remained.

Behind the screen he gave the woman a quick examination which was punctuated by moans and vociferous complaints, and could find nothing to warrant such a fuss. Her huge body was bruised and her heart action was rapid but that was not to be wondered at considering the way she was acting. Once she attempted to snatch the stethoscope from the doctor's hands but he was too quick for her. They glared at each other for a long moment before he turned to Judith. His eyes were hard and his rather full lips had become a thin line. He looked as if he were about to show his teeth in a snarl of anger.

"We'll take her out of here, Morley," he snapped. "She belongs in a psychopathic ward—if we had one. The woman's on a temper jag. We'll put her in the Jensen room. Well—get the orderlies, can't you?"

Judith flushed. He had never spoken so to her before. How dared he! Her head was high as she moved to the door to press the button that would summon the orderlies. She pressed it repeatedly. She was hurt and angry. Two orderlies hurried into the ward. Doctor Booth looked disgusted but it required not only their services but those of Doctor Booth and Judith as well to transfer the irate, noisy woman to the isolated room down the hall.

The Jensen room was separated from the other rooms on the floor by the elevators and the fifth floor linen room and was reserved for just such cases as this. Husky Janet Cameron, the floor nurse, took over.

The windows were graying with the first signs of daylight before the ward became quiet. Such a night! Both nurses were exhausted when relief came at seven.

"No breakfast for me this morning, Morley, or chapel either," Amy said as she went toward the elevator with weary, plodding feet. "I'm going to take a hot bath and slide into bed and if anyone disturbs me before five this p.m., I'll murder 'em. Oh, why, oh why, did I ever get into this mess? Why didn't I stay on the farm?"

"I'm going for a walk," Judith said. "I've got to get out out of here and get some fresh air. I'm not hungry and I don't think I could sit and listen to Winters intone the morning lesson right now. This is one time when I feel anything but religious. That woman! I can hear her voice even yet."

The girls parted at Judith's door. She removed her cap and slipped on a coat. She supposed she should have changed her shoes and uniform. Winters didn't approve of the nursing staff appearing on the street in any part of their hospital uniform. Silly, Judith pronounced, but conformed to the extent of discarding her cap and donning a coat instead of her scarlet-lined blue cape which she admired. It was comfortable and becoming. So many of Winters' rules were ridiculous; but even while they scoffed, the girls obeyed them—to some extent.

Judith usually enjoyed morning chapel. She found the reading of the psalms at once soothing and stimulating, comforting and inspiring. But this morning she felt stifled and in need of air.

The day was anything but pleasant. A chilly wind made her button her coat and step out briskly. The sun was hazy and seemed to lack warmth. Perhaps she needed a cup of coffee. She should have stopped for breakfast even if she wasn't especially hungry. She felt she wanted to avoid talk —the chatter of the breakfast table. She tried to make herself believe it was all due to Mrs. Luini and her tantrum;

but she knew it was having Larry Booth appear when she was expecting the resident. Having him treat her as if she were a stranger—even one whom he disliked. She knew the other girls were curious. Isabelle Carey had even ventured the remark that she was well rid of him—she had never liked him, anyway. Brenda Newton had looked sympathetic but being on rather more than friendly terms with the rapidly recovering Linus Porter, was walking on air. Judith wondered how his mother liked that. She would enjoy telling Mrs. Porter that her precious son could never hope to do better.

The brisk walk in the sharp spring air was beginning to increase her hunger. She remembered that neither she nor Amy had eaten their two o'clock lunch. Between Mrs. Luini's yells and the tears and angry protests of the other women, the two nurses found no leisure in which to eat. By the time the ward was again quiet, the coffee was cold and all desire for food had vanished.

"What Cranford Memorial needs is an eight-hour law," Judith said to herself as she walked on, her gray eyes searching for a place to eat. "Twelve hours is altogether too long a stretch, especially in the wards. Most hospitals have eight-hour shifts; but Cranford just won't be modernized—anyway, not while Winters is superintendent."

She passed a restaurant, paused, retraced her steps and went in. The place was well filled with men and women, most of them reading the morning paper. The appetizing odor of hot coffee, fresh bread, ham and eggs, made her almost ill. She found a table near the back of the big room and sat down. A hand was raised in salute and a tall, red-headed young man came over to her table and pulled out the chair opposite. There was no answering smile to his gay greeting.

"What rotten luck!" she thought.

"Good morning, Judy," Rufus Grant said as he sat down and eyed the sober face before him with concern. "What's wrong? You look like the end of a hard winter. Night duty still, I take it. Why aren't you in bed?"

"I needed a walk and came out without breakfast. I wasn't hungry when I left. What brings you to town this early and during the spring planting, my friend?" she asked and turned to give her order to the waiter.

"I was sitting over there near the window when I ordered," Rufus explained to the man. "Bring my order to this table, please."

His order came almost at once. Judith's eyes glowed hungrily as she view the plate of ham and eggs, hot rolls and steaming coffee the waiter set before him. Rufus grinned at her.

"Why, Judy, you're famished!" he exclaimed. "Here, you take this and I'll have yours when it comes. Go right ahead. I'm a fast eater."

"But I ordered just coffee and toast," she remonstrated, her greedy eyes on the plate he was shoving toward her.

"No meal for a working woman," he told her and Judith accepted his offer and began her breakfast.

When the waiter arrived he was scandalized. Judith laughed and explained.

"The gentleman is not hungry and I am."

"But—but you ordered this. I have it right here—this——"

"Don't mind her, George," Rufus told him. "You may leave this and I'll nibble on it while you duplicate my first order—ham and eggs—make it two, sunny side up—hot rolls, coffee, and I'll have more cream if you please. Make it snappy if you can."

"Thank you, sir," the pseudo George murmured and departed.

"This is good!" Judith exclaimed as she spread butter on a bit of hot roll. "These rolls are really hot. I've never been in this place before."

"No? I stop here every time I come to town. It's pretty decent."

"Pretty decent? It's perfect!" Judith declared emphatically.

The room was fast emptying. Judith supposed all these

people worked in offices downtown. The girls were groomed. Yes, they must all have office jobs. The shops began work much earlier. She was amazed to find her plate suddenly empty.

"I had no idea I was so completely starved," she explained, feeling almost apologetic.

"Oh, have another cup of coffee and maybe a cooky or a friedcake," he urged. "Keep me company. It's the least you can do after eating my breakfast," he teased, trying to ease the tension he felt she was under.

"But my figger!" Judith replied. "I've eaten a huge meal—more than I've ever eaten at this time of day. Usually my breakfasts consist of just what I ordered here— except that I start with orange juice—which more often than not is mostly water."

"No wonder you reminded me of a hungry child when you came in, my dear. Breakfast should be your best meal—shows you have lots of pep and vitality. Ah, heie comes my breakfast at last. How does it appeal to you now, Judy?"

Judith shook her head. "Please don't hurry, Rufus— honestly," she remonstrated as he began to eat, "you must have been as hungry as I was." She looked at her watch and stood up. "Gracious, it's nearly nine! I must get back."

Rufus put out a hand as she attempted to pass him and got to his feet. She was promptly reseated and ordered to wait for him. He had his car outside and would drive her back. Maybe they could even take a short ride. He spread butter lavishly on a piece of roll and gazed at her with anxious brown eyes.

"What's troubling you, Judy?" he asked softly. "I know something is and—you know—well, maybe I can help." At the sudden chilling of the girl's manner he said hurriedly: "Look, the sun!"

As if a curtain had been lifted, the room was flooded with radiance. Rufus' eyes glowed with pleasure and he turned his face to the window. "It's going to be a fine

85

day after all, Judy. Couldn't you come on out to the farm with me this morning? It's only twelve miles and it would do you all sorts of good—just to get away for a few hours. Couldn't you manage it? I'd get you back in time to go on duty at seven.

"And get no sleep, I suppose," Judith pointed out, feel at the moment very wide awake and as if sleep were the farthest thing from her mind.

"You could take a nap. Mrs. Jeffrey would see you're not disturbed and believe me you will taste some of the finest food you've ever had. Jules is a swell cook if I do say so." His plate was empty and he swallowed the last of his coffee. "How about it? Will you do it? I'll take that," as Judith's check was placed beside her plate.

"Of course not," she told him, getting determinedly to her feet. A sudden thought struck her. She sat down again. "If you have such wonderful food at your place how come you're eating breakfast in Nottingham this morning? I'll have that check, please."

"Don't you be silly," he said, ignoring her outstretched hand. "You see, I spent the night at my brother's. Bernice Cranford gave a dinner dance last night and I couldn't seem to get out of going."

Judith froze. So that was why Larry was so cranky— sore at the whole world. Maybe he hadn't been invited or perhaps he had been compelled to leave early. As if he had read her thoughts, Rufus said:

"Doctor Booth was out of luck last night. It seems your resident—Branch, I think they called him—was summoned to the bedside of a sick relative. Doctor Cranford ordered Booth to take over, which, I fancy, didn't set so well with either Bernice or the handsome doctor. Think that will be a match, Judy?" he asked tentatively, his eyes searching her face.

"Maybe," she answered non-committally. "It would be a fine thing for him," she added. "Doctor Cranford could do a lot for him."

"And do you suppose that fact might weigh rather heavily with Larry Booth, Judy?"

Again Judith stood up. "I haven't the least idea," she said coldly. "Bernice Cranford is very beautiful and—oh, I've got to hurry."

"No, you haven't got to hurry," he contradicted as he followed her to the street. He opened his car door and helped her in. "I'm going to take you up to Hill-top Plateau, Judy," he explained as they sped through Nottingham. "There's something about the view from the plateau that sort of quiets a person—sweep away the cobwebs and makes one realize how trivial the worries and cares of everyday life really are after all. From the Rest House one can see into five counties and catch the shimmer of three lakes."

"How far is it?" Judith asked.

"Only somewhere in the neighborhood of six miles—to the top. We could buy provisions and cook our dinner up there if you like——"

"Oh, no. Not today. Sometime maybe, Rufus. Don't let's go today. Let it be some day when I'm in the mood. I'm terribly tired—isn't there a shorter drive——"

"Sure. Dozen of them. Now relax, Judy. Leave everything to me. Forget the hospital and the staff—particularly the staff—and concentrate on something more pleasant."

"Okay. But we must not be too long. I'm doing ward duty—women's ward—and believe me we have a full quota just now. I wonder why it is that spring seems to fill Cranford to its doorstep."

"I think I'll take a week or two over there. It might do me good at that. At least I'd get some attention—more than I get now. Relax, girl!" he reiterated. "You're too tense. We'll turn here for the lake road. It's a pretty drive. We'll see men plowing, see the trees beginning to show signs of returning life and busy housewives starting their spring housecleaning. Do you know, to me, one of the most interesting and compelling signs of spring is the

87

annual beating of rugs, the airing of bedding and clothes lines filled with blowing curtains. I grow almost lyrical at the sight."

Judith laughed skeptically. "I bet you never actually experienced a real housecleaning orgy in your whole life, Rufus Grant. If you had you'd feel anything but lyrical at its semi-annual approach. It's positively deadly. I don't hold with it. I would ban the custom if I had my way."

"Tut, tut, girl. And you a trained nurse! Don't you believe then that cleanliness is next to godliness?"

Judith knew he was trying to divert her thoughts from Larry Booth and the hospital—especially Larry. She was ashamed that the need of diversion was so obvious. Where was her vaunted serenity—her hard realism—her common sense? She spoke seriously.

"Of course I agree, Rufus, but what I can't understand is why confine it to just one or two specific dates—spring and fall? It's like the historic Saturday night bath. House-cleaning is just as outmoded. One's house should be clean at all times."

"Gosh. Judy!" the man cried enthusiastically. "What a wife you're going to make! Think of not having to move out of the house each spring and fall. Come out and sell the idea to Mrs. Jeffrey. It's great, it's colossal! I'm all for it. Say you'll be mine, darling."

"Don't be foolish," Judith said disdainfully. "I'm no housekeeper. I'm a nurse and I ought to be back in my room getting all the sleep I can. Honestly, Rufus, you're sweet to bother about me; but you'll have to turn back. I really must get to bed." She yawned quite realistically— patting her mouth and blinking her eyes in an exaggerated display of drowsiness.

Obediently, Rufus turned the car at the first driveway and they sped back to town. The young man's face settled into grim lines and Judith wondered if she had hurt him. He asked for no future date and, perversely, Judith was annoyed that he didn't, although she told herself that at this time of the year he was probably extremely busy—just as all farmers were. But he found the time to attend Bernice Cranford's parties. Well, let him. No doubt he too had fallen for her blonde loveliness. So her goodbye was cool as she left him and went up to her room in the nurses' home. She was more depressed than when she left it earlier in the morning. Life was a mess. The future looked drab and unexciting—just a continuous round of giving alcohol rubs, taking temperatures and hiding behind a mask of serene efficiency.

She followed Amy Ingham's example. Took a hot bath and crept into bed. For a time she tossed and turned, finding it difficult to compose herself to sleep. Kaleidoscopic scenes flashed before her closed eyes. Her mind seethed with tormenting thoughts. Was Larry actually in love with Bernice Cranford or was it the chief who was engineering the whole affair? How could he have changed so completely? It was scarcely a month since he swore he loved her—wanted her to marry him.

How right Aunt Hepsie had been! Leeds women were unlucky. Love was not for them. Love had been their undoing. And men—men had never been true to them. Well, she had all the rest of her life to get used to the idea and she might as well begin right now. She sat up in her narrow bed, hands about her knees, and brooded over a future devoid of Larry Booth. It looked dark and cheerless. She punched her pillow and lay back, her thoughts unaccountably switching to the man she had just parted from. She smiled as she recalled the breakfast she had eaten—his breakfast. Rufus was sweet. She stretched lazily and relaxed, breathing slowly and rhythmically, trying to empty her mind of every thought until at last she slept.

CHAPTER EIGHT

No DOUBT it was the Easter benefit dance just two days off that caused Cranford Memorial Hospital to take on an air of suppressed excitement. That made little groups of laughing, whispering nurses gather in corridors and outside safely closed doors. That drove Addie Turner, the telephone operator, to hold her head and declare she was getting out of this madhouse before she completely lost her mind. The patients caught the spirit and many of them took a keen interest in what their particular nurses were going to wear and the names of their escorts. That is, the women patients, who were not too ill, wanted this. The male population was bored or frankly disapproving. Nurses had no business staying up all night dancing when next day there would be sick people depending on them for care. It wasn't right.

Judith had about decided not to attend. She was off duty for forty-eight hours and decided she would run out to see Mrs. Leeds. One of her nurses had written her that the old lady would probably not last through the summer. Anyway, there was no one with whom she cared to go. In fact, no one had invited her although she realized it was partly her own fault. Luther Gates had made one or two suggestive hints that she knew were meant to convey the idea he wanted to escort her. Well, she wouldn't go with him. She was all through with internes, doctors and men in general. She had received a card postmarked Chicago from Rufus Grant. He had told her some time before of his intention to visit an exhibit and take in the convention being held there. So of course he was out of the reckoning. But probably he wouldn't have asked her anyway. She sighed. What could she expect? She had been consistently turning down his invitations. After all, one couldn't expect a man to endure snubbing forever, no matter how often he professed devotion and understanding.

This was the one real party Cranford Memorial had during the entire year. She hadn't gone last year although both Isabelle and Brenda had urged her to go with them and their swains. They had reported it the most fun of anything they had attended and laughed impishly at the fact that they as well as most of the other nurses had refused to do more than lend their presence. They took the stand that it was the Board's party—let the Board ladies do the work. The nurses were far too busy to wait on table, sell tickets or entertain guests. If the Hospital Board was disgruntled, there was little they could do about it.

This year, however, the party was to be held at the Country Club. The Nottingham Women's Club was sponsoring it. Mrs. Richard Stacy was Chairman and Mrs. Stacy insisted on having a member of the nursing staff as one of her assistants. She would make her choice. Everyone refused beforehand. And then Judith received a note. Mrs. Stacy would appreciate her help. Isabelle and Brenda urged her to send regrets. Isabelle knew something of what would be expected of anyone crazy enough to accept Mrs. Stacy's invitation to aid her. The woman was a zaney. Judith would get no thanks for wearing herself out chasing after her. But Judith felt that it couldn't be so bad. She didn't need an escort if she did that. She would go early and could leave early. She would see everyone who attended and could be in the party but not of it.

So she accepted Mrs. Stacy's invitation and tried on the two evening dresses she owned, one after the other; did her hair in four different ways, decided to wear it as she always did and on the afternoon of the dance, hurried over to Pierre's for a shampoo and wave-set when the man was swamped with customers. But Judith had nursed Pierre's little daughter through an appendectomy and Pierre would have turned handsprings for her.

Back at the nurses' home she slipped into her gown and stared at her reflection in her mirror. Why did she care so much about this particular party? Why did she want to look her best—to look beautiful? She couldn't fool herself. Larry Booth would be there with Bernice Cranford. But he wouldn't give so much as a glance at Judith Morley.

Well, she didn't care—she wanted to show him she wasn't hurt—that she had never taken him seriously. For a moment the gray eyes gazing back at her grew bleak and the mobile lips drooped.

"Whew! You're certainly a knockout, Judy," Isabelle Carey exclaimed as Judith turned in answer to the other's knock. "I wish I could go right now, too, instead of waiting for Dick."

"Dick? How come? What's Carter doing tonight?" Judith asked.

"Lecturing over at Milford General. Dick flew to Washington this morning on some fool errand and won't be back until late—if ever. That lug gets balmier by the minute. Anyway, I'll be along sometime. Have a lot of fun, Judy. You might try putting cyanide in Winters' coffee. That dame gets in my hair—cuss her!"

"Forget her," Judith advised. "When I'm away from this place I refuse to think about it or anyone in it. I'm not a nurse tonight, Isabelle."

"Don't be infantile. You're a nurse all right. Ma Stacy wouldn't have asked you if you weren't. You'll never be allowed to forget it—not for a second. Why, all the hospital big-bugs will be there—even the stuffed shirts from the University over in Milford, not to mention all the Board ladies—don't forget them. Take it from me, they're the worst. What are you supposed to do? I thought maybe you'd even wear your uniform."

Judith looked nonplused for a moment. "I was asked to assist Mrs. Stacy," she explained a bit doubtfully.

"Sure," the other agreed. "You'll assist her all right. I bet a dollar she won't let you out of her sight. But if she's still got you tied to her apron strings when Dick and I arrive, we'll rescue you. After all, you're not being paid to work there, are you? Or does she consider the invitation remunerative enough? Sorry you have but one life to give for dear old Cranford. Well, s'long, darling. Be seeing you."

The door closed and Judith stood irresolute. She had

half a mind to telephone Mrs. Stacy—telling her she couldn't possibly make it—that she was ill—dead. She took off her wrap. There came a knock on the door. The maid reported the Stacy car was waiting to take Miss Morley to the Club. Judith went downstairs. Maybe Isabelle was spoofing. How did she know so much about what was expected of her?

But of course she did. The Easter benefit dance was an old story to her. Perhaps that was why she refused to help.

Her knees were shaking as she got out at the Club and walked up the broad shallow steps to the front door. There were a few people scattered about in the big hall and they stared admiringly at Judith. She had been here before and she went up the elaborate staircase to the powder room, hoping to find Mrs. Stacy. The room was empty, not even the colored maid who cared for their wraps and made herself generally useful to the guests was in evidence. But of course it was early.

She sat before the mirror getting more panicky by the minute. What was she supposed to do? Where was everyone? She wished she hadn't come. Footsteps hurried along the hall and paused at the door.

"Oh, here you are," a pert voice exclaimed after a moment in which the owner of the voice had examined the girl inside the room. "All dressed up. I hardly knew you, Miss Morley." Angela Stacy came to perch on the arm of a chair there to inspect the girl at the dressing-table. "I like your hairdo. Pierre?"

Judith nodded, powdering her nose. "I like it—sort of. It's different."

"Makes you look like an adventuress. Mother won't like it. She's all for beauty unadorned, if you know what I mean. You look so different without your cap. I don't think I ever saw you without it before." She came nearer and touched the soft waves of dark hair with exploring fingers.

"What am I supposed to do—help your mother, I know; but how?" Judith asked.

"Oh, she'll tell you, don't worry. Come on, if you're ready. Let's go downstairs. Mother and about a thousand other women are in the small dining room."

Judith followed Angela's flying feet in their gilt slippers. She longed to ask about Rufe but thought better of it. Angela was a queer girl and might consider the inquiry presumptuous. Judith's chin lifted. She didn't intend to take any patronizing from these people. She had graciously accepted the invitation to assist in this charity dance—well then. Let anyone just dare to try to patronize her!

Mrs. Stacy looked up from the cards she was sorting to smile a greeting at Judith. The mild blue eyes examined the girl before her and a puzzled frown puckered her brow.

"Don't be a goon, Mother!" Angela hissed impatiently. "It's Miss Morley—you know—my nurse."

Mrs. Stacy put out her hand and took Judith's. Of course, my dear, of course," she fluttered. "You look so different—so—well, you look like everyone else—no—forgive me, I'm in such a dither over this dance. I always say I'll never be chairman of anything again and then I find myself going all through it—having the same trouble. I'm very glad you could come, my dear. You're so dependable—Doctor Cranford says. Now this is what we must do——"

The others in the room drifted in and out. Judith listened to the rambling instructions Mrs. Stacy gave her and wondered how on earth she was going to follow them. Mr. Stacy came in and his wife announced they must have dinner at once. They would be far too busy to eat after the crowds began to arrive.

"I've ordered dinner to be served us right here, my dear," Mr. Stacy said. "It will be along directly. How do you do, Miss ——"

He looked at Judith, his eyes blank, and Judith knew she was an utter stranger to him. People drifted back— the rest of the committee, Judith supposed. Tables were set—some ten or a dozen of them—dinner was served and everyone ate hurriedly. It was fantastic to Judith. There

94

was chatter, laughter, jokes and instructions all rolled into that brief dinner hour. Everything was cleared away before the first arrivals.

"The punch bowl," Mrs. Stacy murmured, staring with unseeing eyes at Judith. Judith wondered what she was supposed to say to that. "Yes, yes, my dear, the punch bowl—very effective—the background—everything—gown —yes, yes. Take the alcove, my dear. Press that button— oh dear—where is it? It was there. I saw it." she pulled aside draperies and at last discovered the electric button in the window casing. "Press this button when the punch is getting low or you need ice or anything. I'm so glad you could come, my dear—call me—if —— Now I must run. You understand?"

Mrs. Stacy drifted away still murmuring to herself. Judith took her place in the alcove behind the table supporting the huge bowl of fruit punch and after a few minutes decided the silver and crystal vessel contained something far more potent than fruit juices. People arrived in droves. Nurses from the hospital came, looking lovely in evening gowns, hailed her commiseratingly and passed on. Brenda stopped to tell her she was an angel to spend the evening stuck away in a corner when every other nurse had refused to do it. Doctor Branch popped in to inquire if she was doing penance and rushed back to the hospital. Someone had to be on deck and he lacked glamor—was too unspectacular to be of much use to anything as ritzy as these parties had grown to be. Judith smiled at him. He might lack glamor but he was one of the finest doctors she had ever known.

Sometimes young men lingered only to be borne off by Mrs. Stacy or another member of the Women's Club. There was a predominance of girls at this party and partners were at a premium. The Women's Club expected every man to do triple duty. Mrs. Stacy fluttered about, came back to the alcove only to hurry away again. She was flushed and excited. The affair was going to be a big success. But never again would she be inveigled into anything of the sort.

"She says that every year," her husband said proudly. "But it seems no one can quite bring it off as Myrtice does."

Judith had seen Bernice Cranford enter with her grandfather and Doctor Booth. She was wearing a filmy green chiffon frock, out of which her perfect head and shoulders lifted like a flower above its calyx.

She smiled graciously right and left, and Larry Booth's eyes were proud and happy as he watched her worshipfully. Doctor Cranford came over to the alcove.

"Good evening, Doctor," Judith said, tearing her tortured gaze from Larry's fatuous face.

"Ah, good evening, Miss—er ——" he replied heartily. Judith was sure he hadn't the least idea of her identity. "Fine crowd tonight. Should go a long way toward rebuilding that wing."

"Mrs. Cranford?" Judith asked. "She isn't here?"

"Oh, no," the chief said regretfully. "She doesn't do much of this sort of thing. I have to, you know—it's expected of me—for the hospital, of course. Yes, one will do a great deal for the hospital."

"You adore it, you old hypocrite!" Judith said to herself. "You love the fuss people make over you and I don't blame them. You really are a dear in spite of your weakness for your granddaughter."

Bernice Cranford and Larry approached the alcove and Judith longed to be somewhere else, anywhere away from the vicinity of these two.

"Is it good, Gramp?" Bernice asked, holding out her hand for a cup. Her blue eyes encountered Judith's cool gaze. "Oh—it's you!" She seemed surprised, though why she should be, Judith couldn't understand.

"Hello, Miss Morley," Doctor Booth said after a moment in which he, too, showed astonishment. Why on earth should they act as if she should not be here? Surely she had a perfect right to help if she wanted to.

"I didn't recognize you out of uniform, my dear," Doctor Cranford said benevolently. "Having a good time?"

Judith laughed softly. "Well, hardly—so far," she confessed.

"I say," the chief announced abruptly, "I'll find someone to spell you and let's you and me make use of this perfectly good music. The Merry Widow Waltz," he mused. "Believe it or not, I was once quite a dancer. Hi there, Mrs.—Mrs. Tanner——"

"Don't be a goose, Gramp," Bernice hissed, catching his arm. "Miss—Miss—this girl is busy here. You can't——"

"Who says I can't? Don't be silly, child," the old man remonstrated. "Come on, my dear—I used to dance this with my daughter—thirty years ago. I don't think I've forgotten. Mrs. Tanner will take Miss Morley's place here at the punch bowl while we have a turn or two around the room. I'll see you get three pillows on your bed when you come to Memorial next time."

Mrs. Tanner laughed and tapped his arm. Bernice glared at Judith who smiled wickedly and floated away in the chief's arms. "You're sweet," she murmured against the old man's coat lapel, but he didn't hear. His head towered above her and he held her rather gingerly. They passed Bernice and Larry. The chief laughed aloud.

"One's offspring can be very stuffy, my dear," he mumured, bending his head. "They have the idea we oldsters are good for nothing but to sit in the chimney corner and dream of bygone days. I'm seventy-two but I'm still very much alive and I've never cared for chimney corners—much. Oh, here comes a young man with determination written all over him. I never did approve of the very rude custom of cutting in, but—you may not, my young friend," he said firmly, and shrugged the hand from his shoulder, whirling Judith out of reach. Judith's heart hammered. But how could it be? He was in Chicago.

The dance ended and Doctor Cranford beamed down at Judith. "That was grand!" the girl said her eyes shining with pleasure. "You're a fine dancer. Now I must go back——"

"Hello, Judy!" someone called from behind and she

knew without turning it was Rufus Grant. Her spirits lifted. "I hoped you would be here; but when I looked for you I couldn't find you."

Judith wondered how he got here.

"I flew back," he said, answering her unspoken question. Rufus was queer that way. She had puzzled over it before. He had an uncanny way of knowing what she was thinking about.

"I've been busy guarding the punch bowl," she told him. "And I must get back to it."

"Who wished that job onto you?" he wanted to know.

"Don't glare at me, Rufus," Doctor Cranford said. "I'm sure I shouldn't have dared."

"I was glad to help," Judith assured him. "Mrs. Stacy asked me."

"I tell you what I'll do, Miss Morley," the chief offered jovially. "I'll take over your job until you feel like coming back. How's that? You and Rufus run along."

"You're a peach, Doctor Cranford," Judith cried while Rufus clapped the older man on the shoulder and pronounced him a brick.

It was some time later that Angela Stacy found a seat beside Judith at the food bar and informed her that her mother was fit to be tied at the way Judith had sneaked out on her. "I told her you were having a good time with Uncle Rufus but it seems you're not supposed to enjoy yourself." The girl laughed impishly. "You're going to catch it, Nursie. Mother can sure put a gal in *her* place."

"Don't be nasty, Angie," Rufus rebuked, "just because you know how."

"You shut up," the girl flared just as young Rufe settled himself beside her. "And don't call me Angie."

"What's up?" the boy asked. "Hi, Unc! What's Angel-face been doing now? I'll have to lock her up—seems like."

"I haven't been doing anything—amiss, Rufe," Angela protested. "My mother invited Miss Morley here to help her. She ran out on her and Mother's wild. That's all there is to it."

Young Rufe eyed Judith for a moment without saying anything. Then he turned to the girl beside him. "Gosh, Angel, your mother didn't expect to keep *her* in the background, did she? And I have always respected your mother's judgment. Why doesn't someone introduce us?" he asked plaintively.

"Miss Morley was my day nurse during the late unpleasantness, Rufe," Angela explained. "The parents liked her so Mother thought that as long as she was supposed to have one of the hospital nurses on her committee, she would ask her. She needn't have accepted the job if she didn't intend sticking to it."

Judith sat silent during the altercation. She had the uncomfortable feeling of being where she shouldn't. Rufus Grant was annoyed and slipped his hand through her arm. "Come on, Judy," he said bruskly. "Let's go some place where people have manners. You should have been spanked thoroughly and often, Angie Stacy, and I'd like to have a whack at you myself. You're a nasty brat and I don't care for you."

"Oh, what does it matter?" Judith spoke calmly. Miss Stacy is right. I should have stuck to my job at the punch bowl." She paused for a moment and couldn't resist saying: "I didn't really want to accept Mrs. Stacy's invitation —I did it because none of the other girls wanted the job. They detest tying themselves down at these affairs; but I like Mrs. Stacy and so I accepted. I'll go and apologize right now."

Angela's face changed. "I wouldn't, if I were you. Mother's feeling imposed upon. I left her sputtering to Doc Cranford while the lovely menace, Bernice, egged her on—figuratively, of course. That Bernice! Larry Booth's a fool to waste his time on her. She'll brush him off one of these days—after he has served her purpose."

"For Pete's sake can the catty chatter, Funny-face," young Rufus admonished. "Miss Cranford's an eyeful, although it takes a man to see it. You'll never get a woman to admire another woman's beauty or what have you. It just isn't in the creatures."

"Nonsense," Judith refuted. "I think Miss Cranford one of the most beautiful girls I have ever seen. I admire her beauty."

"Hip-hip-hip!" Rufe cried, waving his glass aloft. People were staring and Judith longed to get away. Rufus conducted her back to the ballroom where Mrs. Stacy spotted her at once and came bustling forward. Her face was flushed and her eye belligerent. Before she could say a word, Judith murmured:

"I'm sorry if you are annoyed, Mrs. Stacy," she said sweetly.

"Well, I——"

"Oh, come now, my dear lady," Rufus Grant interrupted. "You surely didn't expect Miss Morley to spend the entire evening dishing out punch. I know you didn't. Anyway, Doc. Cranford insisted on her having fun. He insisted—*insisted*, Mrs. Stacy, that Miss Morley let him take over her job."

"I know—I know," Mrs. Stacy agreed. "But you see—well—I have been having the worst kind of luck with my committee tonight. Not one of them is doing the thing for which I invited her. I don't know what——"

"It's a swell party, Mrs. Stacy," Rufus assured her heartily. "Everyone is having a grand time and from the beaming face of Doctor Cranford I'm sure the receipts are generous."

"Oh, the money!" Mrs. Stacy dismissed that subject with a wave of her plump hand. "That part is all right. It's the entertainment——"

"I don't see anything wrong with the entertainment," Rufus said. "The music is good, the food is excellent and the punch terrific, even without Miss Morley ladling it out. What's in it?"

"Why—why, I don't know. The chef mixed it——Oh, Mrs. Welch——Yes, yes—I do thank you, Miss—Miss—

my dear, for helping me out so splendidly tonight. I always say——Have a good time, you two." She slipped her hand through Mrs. Welch's arm and was lost in the crowd.

Rufus laughed. "She's a good soul, although she reminds me of a ship without a rudder most of the time. Come on, let's dance."

Judith shook her head. "I'm going back to the alcove, Rufus," she said firmly. "Doctor Cranford must be bored to tears."

The old surgeon welcomed their return with a twinkle in his eye. "You got a scolding, I see." ·

"Oh, it wasn't bad," Judith assured him. "Thank you for spelling me, Doctor Cranford. Now I'll take over."

Bernice Cranford and Larry Booth joined them. Bernice slipped her hand through Rufus Grant's arm.

"You haven't danced with me once tonight, you bad boy," she murmured, her eyes rebuking.

"He has been otherwise occupied, my dear," the chief laughed as he strolled away to join some of his confrères.

"And so have you been occupied," Rufus told her. "I was late in arriving but what chance would I have had in the crowd that has surrounded you all evening? I couldn't get within yards of you. But how about now?" He held out his arms and she melted into them. Larry Booth frowned and Judith looked away.

"Having a good time?" Doctor Booth asked after a moment. "A big crowd here tonight."

Judith smiled mechanically and agreed there was a big crowd present and was glad when Isabelle Carey and Dick Wilson came over to them.

"Hi ya, Doc!" Dick greeted the young intern. "Surprised to see you in this particular spot," he went on tactlessly. "Ah, the flowing bowl! Now I understand."

"Don't be an idiot," Larry Booth muttered, his eyes glowering. Isabelle laughed. Judith wondered how Isabelle could ever put up with Dick Wilson.

"Having fun, Judy?" Isabelle asked, eying Doctor Booth with veiled dislike.

"Lots of fun, Isabelle," Judith replied.

"I can imagine. How did you let yourself get stuck with this job, anyway?" her friend inquired.

"I don't mind and really I've spent very little time here. The chief took over for more than an hour—in fact he has just left."

"Well, what say Doc here takes over while you come eat with Isabelle and me?" Dick invited. "Go to it, Doc—you'd look swell dispensing refreshments—look the part, too." He grinned maliciously.

"I ate a huge dinner and had a sandwich and coffee just a few minutes ago," Judith explained, making a grimace as she watched Larry Booth vanish in the direction of the group of medical men around Doctor Cranford.

"What's he hanging around you for, Judy?" scowled Isabelle.

"Don't be ridiculous," Judith snapped. "He simply remained where Miss Cranford dropped him."

Dick hooted. "I suppose it petrified him than any gal could drop him even temporarily."

"Me-ow!" jeered Isabelle. "Come on, Dicky, I'm starved. Let's find something to eat. I'll send Brenda and Luther Gates over to relieve you if they're still here."

"Still here?" exclaimed Judith. "What time is it getting to be?"

"Oh, twelve or so. Not late."

"Well," Judith said flatly to empty space, "I'm getting out. I didn't enlist for the duration—merely for the evening. Oh, Miss Stacy!" She beckoned to Angela and Rufe who were passing. "Will you ask your mother to send someone to relieve me, please? I'm leaving."

"Alone?" Angela wanted to know. She was still angry.

"Alone," Judith said firmly. "Does it matter?"

"Not to me it doesn't," Angela said pertly. "I can't vouch for some of the rest of the gals, poor things. Did Mother put you in your place, Miss Morley?"

Rufe lifted his hand and boxed her ears. She turned on him in fury. "How dare you, Rufe Grant? she hissed through clenched teeth. "What business is it of yours?"

Rufe caught her two fists in his and held them firmly. "What ails you, woman?" he demanded. "You act like a hussy. I have a mind to make you apologize to Miss Morley right now."

"You and what dozen others?" Angela raged. "Let go my hands, you—you——"

"Not till you behave yourself," the boy said. "I'm ashamed of you, Angela, and I can't understand why I put up with you and your rotten manners."

Judith was embarrassed. They acted as if she wasn't present. She saw the girl go limp, all anger and pertness drop from her. "Oh, gosh, Rufe!" she whimpered childishly, "I'm sorry. I don't know what makes me so beastly." She turned to Judith and her smile was lovely. "Don't mind me, Miss Morley. I'm just what Uncle Rufus called me— I'm a nasty little brat. But I like you—always have. I guess that's why I'm always trying to get under your skin. You're so—so terribly poised and perfect—it—well, it does something to me."

Judith laughed although she was not in the least amused. "I'm sorry if I affect you that way, Miss Stacy," she said coolly. "And will you please try to find your mother and ask her to send a relief? Thank you." It was dismissal and she saw the wry grimace, quickly suppressed, mar for a moment the beauty of the girl's face.

Judith was depressed and very tired. She wanted nothing so much as the peace and quiet of her room—and bed. It had been a mistake to come. It had proved nothing to her.

Mrs. Stacy appeared almost at once. Timothy, the chauffeur, had been summoned and would take Miss Morley back to the hospital. Mrs. Stacy was shepherding a tall, thin woman who was not only willing but eager to take over the punch bowl. In fact, she was delighted to help dear Mrs. Stacy in any capacity whatsoever. Judith slipped out while the newcomer was still gushing, hoping to escape unseen by either Larry or Rufus Grant.

She got her wrap and sped down the stairs. But she didn't breathe naturally until she was in the Stacy limousine speeding down the drive. She looked back. The huge sprawling building was ablaze with lights. The orchestra was playing another waltz. This time "The Blue Danube." The air throbbed with it. She wondered if Doctor Cranford had found a partner. He loved the old dances. She closed her eyes only to see the look of fatuous devotion on Larry Booth's face as he gazed at Bernice Cranford. Saw Bernice smile provocatively at him while she led Rufus Grant, a willing captive, away from his place beside her in the alcove.

Well, it served her right. She should never have come. Why couldn't she ever seem to listen to the voice of discretion? She was going on night duty in Pediatrics tomorrow—tonight. She was glad it was to be nights—it meant she would be out of circulation—away from temptation. She liked nursing children. She understood them. They got on well together. She settled back against the rich upholstery of the luxurious car and concluded that from this time forward she would stick to her job. She bit her lip to steady its trembling. She must not yield to the insidious weakness of being sorry for herself. She must fight against softness. A wry smile twisted her lips for a moment as she recalled the childish outburst of Angela Stacy: "You're so terribly poised and perfect," she had said. Well, she would go on fooling everyone if—if only she were given another chance—if only she could put Larry Booth completely out of her heart. She would, too. She must if she was to go on living. And then—never again!

The car stopped before the nurses' home. She thanked Timothy as he opened the door for her then hurried up the walk to the porch. The hall light was on. Of course. It wasn't likely many of the girls were back. This was an occasion when late hours were excusable. She ran up the stairs and into her room. She just couldn't talk tonight. She felt as if a weight lay on her heart. She undressed quickly, put out her light, then dropped to her knees beside her narrow bed.

Wordlessly she prayed for strength. How long she knelt there she didn't know. She must have slept for the sound of the ambulance leaving the courtyard below roused her. The east was reddening. Dawn was near. She was stiff and cold; but as she crept into bed and pulled the blanket over her tired body, her heart was somewhat strangely comforted.

She knew nothing more until her alarm went off at seven o'clock. She lay for a while trying to recall the events of the night before. In the light of day it all seemed trivial. Even the memory of Larry's abject and open devotion to Bernice Cranford was as something outside her ken. Rufus Grant had been sweet, but she had no desire to see him again. Angela Stacy was amusing in her childish rudeness and Rufe was a dear.

"It was an experience," Judith told herself wryly. "When life takes a sock at one the only thing to do is to sock it right back. I'm not licked yet. But hereafter I think I'll stick to my knitting.

She went to her dresser and picked up the sign: "DO NOT DISTURB" and hung it outside her door, then crawled back into bed again and fell instantly to sleep.

CHAPTER NINE

HEARD THE NEWS, Judy?" Isabelle Carey asked one wet May afternoon when they met in the almost deserted gymnasium.

"What news? I haven't heard a thing since I've been in Pediatrics. It seems sometimes as if I'm being shunned by my fellows—or as if I had some terribly contagious disease. What ails you all? And tell me how you and Carter are making out and Brenda and her gall bladder?"

"Then you have heard?" Isabelle countered. "I just wondered."

"I don't know what you're talking about," Judith insisted, a spasm of pain clutching at her heart. So it was about Larry—he was going to marry Bernice Cranford. That was it—she had known it was coming. Now it was here.

"Do you mean that?" Isabelle asked, scanning the face of the girl before her with troubled eyes. "Didn't you know the engagement had already been announced —days ago and the wedding is to be right away—in June? Fast work, I calls it. But marrying in haste give one more leisure for repentance and believe me the handsome Larry'll have plenty of repenting to do even if he gets little leisure."

The huge room spun around Judith for a moment before she could bring herself to speak. When she did so she was astonished at the coolness of her voice.

"There must be something to this 'love at first sight' business, Isabelle," Judith smiled. "It seemed to strike him like a bolt from the blue. I suppose his job as assistant to the chief is assured?"

"Of course," her friend said and gave an audible sigh of relief. She turned her back and bent forward invitingly. "Give me a good swift kick, Judy," she ordered. "I've been breaking my heart over you and that penny-halfpenny bloke and here you're as calm as a cucumber. Go on, darling. I can take it and I sure have it coming to me."

Judith laughed. "Don't be a nut, Isabelle," she said, turning a summersault and landing on her feet in front of the other. "I've told you a hundred times if I have once that Larry Booth and I were just good friends. I'm not interested in men—never have been."

"Ya-ah," Isabelle murmured skeptically, "I've heard them there sentiments expressed before and they don't mean a darned thing. But tell me. How about the red-headed Grant chap?" she asked. "He's a persistent cuss for one who receives no encouragement. Why don't you like him, Judy?"

"Oh, I do like Rufus," Judith assured her, "but—well—I'm never going to tie myself down with any man——"

"Horsefeathers!" Isabelle interrupted scornfully. "D'you mean to stand there and tell me you don't intend to marry —ever?"

"Just that, Isabelle," Judith said calmly.

"But why?" the other asked.

Judith shrugged slim shoulders. "It's just that I don't care for men," she said.

"But you could if you would let yourself go," her friend told her earnestly. "Be yourself—forget your inhibitions."

"Don't hand me that line," Judith snapped.

"It isn't a line. It's the truth. Is it because of Larry Booth, Judy? I don't care. I'm going to say it and you can shake your head and freeze me all you like. You listen to me, Judy Morley. I'm not trying to pry and if you say you never cared for him it's all right with me—I'll believe you—with reservations," she finished *sotto voce* and if Judith heard she made no sign. "But this Rufus Grant is a horse of a different color entirely. He's real —all wool and a yard wide. I've heard some definitely nice things about him and he's certainly the fulfilment of a gal's dream—a normal, sensible gal, I mean. I wish I had a chance there. Believe me, I'd jump at it even if I wasn't head over heels in love with him. I could easily learn to be. He's a prince and there's something vitally wrong with a girl who turns him down."

"Rufus is all you say he is, Isabelle," Judith agreed, "but I still say I'm not marrying anyone—anyone at all —ever. Now please let's change the subject. How is Brenda getting on with Linus Porter? He must have gone home before this, hasn't he?"

"Gone home!" the other exclaimed. "Gosh, girl, you have been out of things! He's not only gone home but gone to Arizona as well. Ma carried him right after he left here. Brenda is going around like a ghost although she told me he had written her several letters; but if he's like most men, those letters have been far from satisfactory. I don't know, Judy, but sometimes I'm afraid Brenda is in for a heartache—many heartaches. She fell so completely for that boy and from what I can find out he's one of these here lads with a mother complex—a mama's boy. It's a rotten shame. Brenda's such a sweet kid. If he turns her down I hope some she-devil gets hold of him who'll put crimps in Ma Porter's spine. Carter's an orphan—that's why I'm out to land him."

Judith had been laughing but she quickly sobered. "Being an orphan isn't any fun, Isabelle," she said.

"Maybe not in some cases, but believe me many mothers-in-law play havoc with an otherwise happy marriage. I know. Your red-head is an orphan, Judy. You'd have none of that to contend with. Listen. Why don't you give the chap a break? Why let everyone think you're wearing weeds for Larry Booth—the lug! Why inflate his already bursting ego still more? I'm sorry, darling," she said hastily. "I'm a fool for shooting off my mouth. But just the same, the advice is good and you could do much worse than follow it."

Judith's face had been a study in changing expressions as her friend talked. Now she forced a smile. "Thanks," she said, mockingly. "Your wide experience has made advice from you invaluable. I'll think about it."

Isabelle refused to take offense. "You'd better," she

advised. "It makes my blood boil to see that smarty-pants strut around giving orders and staring holes in my back when I fail to heed them. He certainly gets my goat."

"Oh, forget him, Isabelle!" Judith protested. After all, he's going to be here a long time and——"

"Well, we needn't be and what's more I don't intend staying on much longer—if I can only work Hank to the proper point. He's wary, that guy; but he's warming up. He's got a chance at a practice over in Beaumont. I'm all for it. He'll never get anywhere in this town. Old Dalton will live forever and doesn't hold with the idea of retiring. Why, Judy, Doctor Dalton must be nearly eighty."

"Oh, I don't think he's that old," Judith laughed. "Seventy-two or three, perhaps, but surely not eighty."

"Just the same I'm encouraging Hank to follow up the Beaumont lead. It's a grand little town. We drove over there on one of my afternoons off and I even picked out the house I want."

"You did? And Hank? What about him?"

"Oh, he thought it was all right but rather large for a bachelor. I could have screamed. Bachelor indeed! He'll not go to Beaumont a bachelor if I have anything to say about it. I'm serious this time, my girl, and when I mean business something's bound to happen. Pray for me."

"I will," Judith promised. She felt sure Isabelle was only half in earnest; that she was putting on an act for her especial benefit. She didn't believe for a minute that her friend accepted her assertion that she cared nothing for Larry Booth—hadn't been hurt by his defection. Now she slipped her hand through Isabelle's arm and they walked to the stairs leading to the gallery beyond which was the nurses' home. "But you don't need my prayers, darling," she said confidently. "Neither Hank Carter nor any other man could resist you for long—that is if you want him. I'm excepting no one."

"Listen to her!" the other scoffed. "I'm no beauty

and no great shakes as a woman either. I know my faults and believe it or not, Judy Morley, inside I'm an arrant coward. I have to force myself to do things. My parents were divorced and I was brought up by my grandmother, one of those straight-laced Victorian females, a perfect lady who disapproved of everything I did in general principles and never forgave her daughter, my mother, for dragging the family honor through the courts in spite of the fact, mind you, that she hated my father. She died and left me at loose ends. Not enough money to live on in style to which her annuity had accustomed me, and with my mother somewhere abroad and my father— Heaven knew where. Well, I took my life into my own hands and went to business school for a year. My first job showed me pretty conclusively that I wasn't the material from which business wizards or office wives are made. One of my pals entered a hospital training school and I followed suit. The first six months I lived in constant dread of being found out. Of openly rebelling at some of the stuff expected of me; of exposing my cowardice—my fear of death and my squeamishness and false modesty in caring for patients. Gran had made a poor, white-livered craven of me and I want to tell you that nine years in a hospital hasn't cured me. Oh, I put up a good front— my armor seems to be impregnable; but believe me, Judy, I've had to bolster my chin and pray hard to keep going." She laughed raggedly. "They tell me I'm a fine nurse—"

"And you are," Judith interrupted, having a queer feeling in discovering that she and Isabelle Carey were fundamentally so alike.

"I know," the other agreed. "I love my work and yet I hate it. I suppose you can't understand that."

"But I can," Judith said. "There are times when I feel much the same way and wonder why on earth I ever took up nursing. It's a hard life—not too well paid. Its advantages are greatly overrated and one's efforts are so often unappreciated. And yet, there is nothing else I would rather do—even if I were trained for it."

"O-oh," Isabelle said as they paused before her door. "But you're so gifted—so well-equipped. You'd make a glamorous hostess, Judy. You have beauty, poise and style. You would glorify the Grant menage."

Judith hooted derisively. "Rufus Grant is a farmer, Isabelle," she told her.

"I know that's what he claims to be. Did you ever see his farm, Judy?" and as Judith shook her head she exclaimed. "Well!"

"Not interested," Judith retorted, and went down the hall to her own room, followed by Isabelle's warning.

"Mark my words, girl, you'd better be."

Judith entered her room and closed the door. She dressed slowly, pondering the news she had heard. One thing was certain, she could not stay on here at the hospital after Larry became permanent assistant. And yet, if she left now, wouldn't he know that she cared? Well, she did, didn't she? Her hands paused and she sat down in the nearest chair, her knees suddenly weak. She stared at her reflection in the mirror and was startled at the change that had come over her within the past few weeks. She looked thinner and her eyes had lost much of their sparkle.

"No—no," she exclaimed aloud. "It's because of all this night work. It's because I have been worried over Rosemary Logan. It has nothing to do with Larry Booth. That's all past—I—I refuse to give it a single thought."

She finished dressing and went downstairs. She would have time to get to the park and back before dinner. Somehow she felt she must keep away from the telephone, just as she avoided going downtown. She had no desire to see or hear from Rufus Grant just now. That was one good thing about night work. Rufus was usually busy days. She walked along briskly, breathing in the damp air smelling of wet earth and fresh growing things. It wasn't raining now. The west was brightening. Probably going to be a fine evening. What a night for a long ride in the country. Well, not for her. She would be

111

putting children to bed, listening to their complaints and last minute demands while other more fortunate girls were riding in a swank new roadster listening to a man's thrilling voice as he told her what a wonderful wife she would make——What a fool she was! Would she never learn?

Upon her return to the hospital she paused at the bulletin board more from force of habit than because she expected to find anything of interest posted there. It was late and she scanned the closely typed notices hastily. So she was to leave Pediatrics to nurse 273—days. She inquired about the occupant in 273 to find it was Mrs Damerest. A case of nerves—or heartbreak. Well, Judith felt she could sympathize with her. She went on up to her room and changed into uniform. The dining room was nearly empty when she came downstairs and her dinner was anything but satisfactory. Well, she didn't care—much. She would have a long evening in her room and go to bed early. She left word with the maid that she was not to be dsiturbed—under any circumstances. She was out if anyone called.

If anyone did, she didn't know it. She was sorry to leave tiny Rosemary Logan just now that she was out of danger, but glad she hadn't been changed before the improvement was definite. Just why the superintendent saw fit to shift her over to day duty was a mystery to Judith unless pressure had been brought to bear. But whose pressure? Surely Rufus wouldn't interfere even if he did have influence as he professed. She had asked him not to, hadn't she? Well, then.

She pinned her cap in place, turned to see that the seams of her white stockings were quite straight, and opened the door of her room.

"Well, well, who have we here?" Isabelle Carey greeted her blithely. "How come you, too, are to
      " 'Work while the day grows brighter,
        Under the glowing sun'
and so on and on and on?" she sang liltingly. "Whose back are you destined to rub, darling?"

"273—Mrs. Damerest," Judith said. "Where are you?"

"Receiving—no less. Well, at least it's a change from the eternal night work. I'm good and sick of it. I don't envy you your job, my girl," Isabelle told her. "Hood says she's not only neurotic but determined to remain so. Nothing physically wrong—purely a mental case. Preserve me from them! What's she got to be neurotic about? I ask you."

"I wouldn't know," Judith confessed. "What has she?"

"She lost her son. Killed by a truck. So what? She isn't the only mother to lose a child. She's not old. There's plenty of time for her to have five or six—if she wants 'em. She has money—a swell husband and beautiful home. I'm afraid I haven't much patience with her kind. I'm glad Winters put you in there instead of me."

"I still don't understand why I was elected," Judith mused as they walked through the long corridor to the dining room.

"I can enlighten you there, my friend," Isabelle said. "It's because of your calm serenity in the face of famine, war and sudden death so to speak. I'd give a good deal to have had your training, Judith Morley."

Judith shook her head. "No, you wouldn't," she said seriously. "I learned in a hard school, Isabelle. But if I can help the poor thing I'm glad I'm to be with her. I'd much rather have night, though. Neurotics are usually much worse at night. Is Hood her night nurse?"

"Good old Hood!" Isabelle murmured. "She certainly gets handed some pretty tough assignments. But the gal's sound—she can take it."

They found places at the long table and were silent until the end of the meal. Talk and laughter went on all about them but Judith and Isabelle were occupied with their own thoughts. They went down the hall to the small chapel side by side. The room was well filled and Miss Winters looked almost human as her cold blue eyes scanned her audience. She opened the Psalter and began reading the Ninety-first Psalm. Her voice was precise and perfectly expressionless. The responses came low but clear, the voice of the chief, seated just behind the superintendent, rising above those of the members of his staff. The Psalm ended. There was a pause while Psalters were laid aside.

"The Lord is my shepherd; I shall not want."
The old familiar words were repeated in unison. Judith closed her eyes. She loved it—it seemed to have been written especially for her.

"Surely goodness and mercy shall follow me all
the days of my life; and I will dwell in the house
of the Lord forever."

"Now I'm ready for my neurotic," she said to Isabelle as they left the chapel. "I don't know why I ever skip these morning services," she went on as they paused beside the elevator. "I always get a lift——"

Isabelle laughed. "You're going to get one now, my hearty," she jibed as she turned toward Receiving. The elevator whined to a stop. Other nurses crowded close. The elevator car accommodated six but eight usually managed to get in at one time, much to the displeasure of the superintendent. Judith's smile followed her retreating friend. Isabelle was like that—avoiding anything remotely resembling sentimentality. Judith knew she should have kept her thoughts to herself. But just the same she felt better.

She got out at the third floor and walked along to 273. The door was ajar and the sound of voices—one dull and listless, the other determindedly cheerful, reached her. She went in. Marie Hood grimaced when she saw her.

"Here comes our very best nurse, Mrs. Damerest," she told the patient brightly. Mrs. Damerest didn't even open her eyes.

Hood shook her head and dropped her hands to her sides in a gesture of futility. Judith picked up the chart and over its meager recordings smiled into the other nurse's tired eyes. She followed her to the door.

"What can one do when the patient just won't cooperate—doesn't want to live?" Hood muttered desperately as she stepped into the corridor. It had been a long, hard case—lasting now well into its second month, with practically no improvement. "Her own doctor thinks she should be in a psychopathic hospital. This morning I agree with him. Branch doesn't—neither does the chief. They insist she's coming along all right. They say she'll snap out of it one of these days—but—oh, my poor head!" She held the offending head with both hands.

"Go out for a walk, Hood," Judith advised. "That usually fixes me up after a particularly hectic night. Stop some place downtown for breakfast and you'll see you'll feel lots better when you come back."

She smiled to herself as she closed the door after the departing night nurse. She recalled doing that very thing not long before and meeting Rufus Grant. But even though Hood didn't meet anyone she knew—certainly not Rufus—the brisk walk in the fresh air would without doubt help her aching head.

273 was one of the most expensive rooms in Cranford Memorial—certainly one of the pleasantest. Just now the shades were down but even so sunlight poked experimental fingers along the sides and at the bottom of each window. Judith raised the shade from one window—raised it and the window halfway. The rain of the previous day had filtered the air and the fresh little breeze that fluttered the crisp white curtains brought a breath of growing things into the room. She turned to the patient lying on her back, eyes closed and pale, limp hands curled outside the coverlet. There was something pathetic about her—something almost despairing that caught at Judith's heart.

Mrs. Damerest was a pretty woman in spite of the ravages made by her sorrow and subsequent mental illness. Thirty and already tired of life. But she couldn't be. It was just inertia—too much leisure and too little of real interest. If she had to earn her living—had to fight to keep soul and body together—she would never have fallen into this Slough of Despond. The dark eyes slowly opened only to close again.

"Hello!" Judith said quietly. "Feeling better? Ready for your breakfast? And what appeals to you this morning, Mrs. Damerest? You may have just about anything you like, you know. That's the advantage of not being physically ill. How about a glass of chilled orange juice for a starter and—maybe crisp toast and—marmalade? Our marmalade is very good, or have you tried it? The old lady who makes it is a Scotch refugee, you know. She came over with her two grandchildren. It's the real thing, that marmalade. It's wonderful."

"I couldn't touch a thing," the patient murmured indifferently. "What's your name?" she asked, her eyes still closed, the long dark lashes curling back from her colorless cheeks.

"Judith Morley, Mrs. Damerest." She pressed a button that summoned the patient's breakfast tray and went on. "I've been in Pediatrics for the past few weeks. I wish you could see the youngsters in that ward eat their breakfast. Makes one hungry just to watch them." Judith eyed her patient—expecting the spasm that was supposed to follow each mention of children. She had heard the spell often lasted hours. Why, it really wasn't at all bad. Just a slight twitching of the mouth and a frown as of pain and then once more a listless, blank face. Maybe they had all been barking up the wrong tree. Perhaps Mrs. Damerest needed to talk about her son. It might not be amiss to give the idea a trial. She went on her voice rising and falling musically as she told of the tricks the children employed to eat only what they liked. Once Mrs. Damerest murmured:

"I know, Nurse. Tommy hated oatmeal; he—Oh——" She covered her eyes for a moment then let her hand drop back to the coverlet.

"There's a little girl over there," Judith continued, watching the other unobtrusively. "She's three years old and absolutely alone in the world. Both parents gone. She's like a sunbeam now that the burns have stopped hurting and she can sit up a part of each day. At first she kept calling her mother; but now she seldom speaks of her except just before going to sleep at night. She's so tiny to lose her mother."

"What's her name?" came from the bed, in a whisper.

"Rosemary Logan. Perhaps you heard of the fire over near the lake? The Logan house was destroyed—and—well, both parents died here in the hospital within an hour of each other. But Rosemary won't be an orphan long, Mrs. Damerest. Already we have had several offers for her adoption. Of course she isn't well enough to leave us yet and the nurses wish they could keep her all the time. She's a beautiful child and wonderfully well trained already. Her mother must have been a fine woman."

"Is she badly scarred?" Mrs. Damerest asked.

"Not at all—except one leg and that is pretty well healed. No doubt whoever adopts her will want to have a bit of plastic surgery done there. It's near the thigh, though—that is, the worst scar is, and I doubt if it will show much even in a bathing suit. If you like, I'll bring her in to see you some day. You'll love her."

"No—no—I can't," the patient cried, pressing her hand to her mouth.

"Oh, not today, Mrs. Damerest," Judith exclaimed. "I meant when you are better—able to sit up I wouldn't want Rosemary to see you in bed—it would probably upset her. Poor little mite—she's had a hard time of it. Now I'm going to give you an alcohol rub and then we'll see if a glass of iced orange juice won't taste good to you."

Mrs. Damerest said nothing and Judith went about the job of massaging her patient's lovely body. "Rubbing their backs," as Isabelle called it derisively. Martha brought her tray and Judith raised the bed, arranging the table so that everything was within easy reach. Flowers began to arrive and she busied herself with arranging them to the best advantage, bringing in those that had been removed for the night and exclaiming over their beauty. She kept an unobtrusive and not too inquisitive eye on the occupant of the bed. The orange juice was almost gone. The toast nibbled at—then a bit spread with marmalade—a second piece larger than the first followed. Judith was jubilant. Just what had aroused this interest in food? Surely she had done nothing to warrant it, or was it the talk about the children? Maybe Mrs. Damerest needed to talk about her boy. Later she would sound her out on the subject.

The resident was pleased when he dropped in later in the morning. He beamed on Judith as if she were the cause of it all and the girl shook her head in protest.

"It was bound to come, Morley," Doctor Branch told her. "Change of nurses evidently helped—especially when the change meant bringing you on the job. You've got something, my girl—something——" His voice trailed off as he hurried down the corridor.

Judith's lip curled derisively. A lot he knew about it.

At ten o'clock Mr. Damerest came to the hospital! He was a tall, thin man in his early thirties with prematurely gray hair and a tragic expression in his blue eyes. He greeted his wife tenderly, his eyes searching her face for some sign of improvement.

"Feeling better, darling?" he asked tentatively, one eye on Judith.

"Not much, Tom," the patient said listlessly.

"But you are going to be, aren't you, Mrs. Damerest?" Judith said positively. "Just as soon as your wife is able to sit up, we are going to have our prize patient pay her a visit. I wish you would stop over in Pediatrics, Mr. Damerest, and introduce yourself to Rosemary Logan—the darling of the ward. No, on second thought, I think we'll save her for your wife. Rosemary's something extra special, you know."

The man was staring at his wife—his eyes fearful. Mrs. Damerest was watching Judith, her expression strange. Judith smiled encouragement at them both.

"She was badly burned, Tom," Mrs. Damerest explained. "Her parents were killed in a fire. Do you remember hearing about it?"

"Of course," the man gulped. "It was just a little

118

while ago. Jim Logan. Sure I remember. It was certainly tragedy all right. Good decent people—the Logans. What will become of the youngster? I thought she died, too." He bit his lip and went on hurriedly, "I suppose she'll have to go to some orphanage?"

"Not Rosemary," Judith said emphatically. "We've had any number of offers to adopt her; but she isn't well enough to leave the hospital yet. Honestly," she laughed, "I think Doctor Branch wants to keep her here—he's mad about her. It woudn't surprise me if he adopted her himself." Judith didn't know any of these things but it made sprightly conversation and seemed to interest her patient.

"But Branch is a bachelor——" Mr. Damerest protested.

"She isn't badly scarred," Mrs. Damerest interrupted as if she hadn't heard.

Abruptly Mr. Damerest stooped to kiss his wife. His eyes were very bright and Judith felt sure he was close to tears. He hurried from the room and Judith followed him into the hall.

"I think we've struck something," she said. "Anyway, it will do no harm to try it."

The man nodded and held up his hand in farewell. Poor chap, he didn't want her to know how he felt—as if she didn't!

A week passed before Mrs. Damerest was able to sit up. She was definitely on the mend. Judith refused to take any credit to herself. Everything was contributing to her recovery. The weather was exceptionally fine. The air was sweet with the scent of growing things and vocal with the song of birds. With the windows of 273 wide to the spring sunshine, one would have to be considerably sicker than Mrs. Damerest to remain unmoved by all the world's loveliness.

On this sunny morning Judith helped her patient to the big wicker chair near a window. She had brushed the soft curly hair until it shone and around the lovely head had tied a wide blue satin ribbon, making a perky bow at one side.

119

"You look like a little girl yourself," she said as she stepped back to view her handiwork. "I wish your husband would walk in right now. He would be mighty proud of you."

"But I'm so dreadfully pale and thin," Mrs. Damerest complained. "And so disgustingly weak."

"But nothing to what you were, my dear. Wait until you have a few more good meals and are able to walk about. Then you'll soon see a real improvement. Now if you're ready, I'll go get Rosemary. She knows all about the pretty lady who has invited her to visit her. She's excited at the prospect. You'll love her."

Judith carried the little girl into the room. Mrs. Damerest held out her hands in welcome. Rosemary demanded to be put down, and walked over to the chair where she stood for a moment examining the smiling girl who sat there, with wide gentian blue eyes.

"Hello!" she said at last. "Have you got any little girls?"

Mrs. Damerest shook her head, her eyes suddenly full of tears. "No," she said softly. "I never had any little girl, Rosemary; but I had a little boy—Tommy——He—he ——" A sob broke from her and she pressed her hand to her mouth.

Rosemary looked up at Judith and then put her hand on Mrs. Damerest's knee. "Don't cwy, dahling," she said in exact imitation of the voice of the resident. "Evwythin's all wite." She patted the knee and smiled up at the anguished face. "All wite," she reiterated stoutly.

Mrs. Damerest caught the child to her and buried her face in the yellow curls. Judith was fearful Rosemary might be frightened but the little girl remained passive, only continuing to murmur: "All wite" in her plaintive baby voice.

"I want her, Miss Morley,'" Mrs. Damerest said at last, lifting drenched eyes. "How would you like to be my little girl, Rosemary?" she asked, smoothing back the sunny hair. "To come home with me and live in my house—all the time?"

Rosemary turned to examine Judith. Her blue eyes looked from one to the other for a long moment. "Will you stay wiv me when it's dark?" she asked. "An' tell me a story an'—an'—can Bwanchy come too an'—an' Judy— an'—an'——"

Judith laughed. "She drives a hard bargain, Mrs. Damerest," she said. "Do you really want to adopt her? But— but—you know there may be—you may have children of your own——"

"No," the patient said sadly. "That's why it was so hard to give Tommy up. There can never be any more. Oh, Tom!" she cried as her husband entered the room. "How do you like our daughter? Say hello to your new daddy, darling."

Rosemary eyed the tall man who had entered and kissed his wife. At last she said shyly: "Hello! Daddy always kissed me, too." She lifted her face and the tall man picked her up in his arms. Judith felt the prick of tears behind her eyelids. She slipped from the room.

Things moved quickly after that. Mrs. Damarest improved as if by magic. The necessary legal steps were taken that made Rosemary Logan Rosemary Logan Damerest and she and her new mother left the hospital together. Judith went back to Pediatrics.

CHAPTER TEN

JUDITH WAS GLAD to return to Pediatrics. Glad, too, to be on night duty. The ward was nearly always well filled, and even though there were several strange faces, it didn't take Judith long to familiarize herself with each new youngster's personal likes and dislikes—all the small tricks and habits that prove a child is an individual. In the very last bed in the long ward lay Philip Conover—twelve years old. He was a newcomer, having arrived two days before Judith returned to the ward. He had fallen from a truck and his back was broken. He had been in a cast forty-eight hours and lay white and tight-lipped in one corner of the room near a wide window from which he could watch the trees and clouds. At least, that was the idea in putting him there.

Judith's heart ached for him—he was so alone—only a stepmother who was resigned to his ultimate death. This in itself seemed horrible to Judith. How could anyone be resigned to the death of a child? Oh. she knew one had to be; but somehow she was never willing to give up. Like Doctor Cranford, she fought to the last. As she looked down at him she forgot her own unhappiness in anxiety over the boy. She had nursed broken backs before—often helping to restore them to health and usefulness. She intended fighting for this youngster—fighting with every ounce of strength, courage and faith she possessed.

It was always hard for a child to become accustomed to a plaster cast but after a while with the adaptability of youth they grew philosophical and made very little fuss. The first day Judith saw Philip she felt sure he had something on his mind. His forehead was clammy, his eyes dark pools of agony.

"It is very bad, Philip?" Judith asked softly, brushing back the thick brown hair from his brow with gentle fingers.

He didn't answer for a moment then he snarled through a corner of his mouth: "What do *you* think? I ain't ever goin' t' git outta here, an' you know it. Don't try t' kid me fer I ain't th' kiddin' sort, see? Now leave me be."

"Who told you that, Phil?" Judith persisted.

"I heard 'em talkin'. I ain't deef. I heard 'em."

"Heard? But whoever it was you heard was probably discussing someone else. You will be here quite a while; but I'm sure you'll come out all right. Doctor Cranford is a very wonderful surgeon, you know. Now cheer up. It's really not so bad here. We have fine times in this ward and you'll like it when you get to know the other children."

"They said: 'The Conover kid,' Miss Nurse. I heard 'em," the lad persisted.

Judith forced a smile. She had to break this dark mood —had to create a determination in this boy to recover— to be strong and well—no matter what the odds.

"You probably heard just a part of the conversation, Philip," she said cheerfully. "You see, I happen to know quite a lot about injured backs—nursed a number of them. One of the small bones in your spine is broken and until it mends you must lie perfectly still. That's why the doctors put you in a cast so the pieces will grow together more quickly. Why, if you didn't have the cast on, you might turn in your sleep and there would be the whole thing to do over again."

The dark eyes devoured her face for a moment, then he spoke again. "How could I turn or move at all with my back broke? Talk sense."

"You couldn't. I meant if the doctors put the pieces together and just left them that way without holding them firmly in place. That's what the cast is for. To hold you firm."

"But I can't even move my legs—they're—they're— they ain't got no feelin's in 'em," he complained.

Judith caught her lip between her teeth and prayed for guidance. "Of course they haven't. They won't have until the bones knit. You'll be able to after a while. Just be patient and watch and when you find you can wiggle your toes, you'll know the broken pieces are growing together all right and you will be out of this armor before you know it. It takes time for old Dame Nature to do her knitting, Phil. She works slowly but surely and does a grand job. So just help all you can by being patient and happy. We're all going to help you."

"Well," Philip said slowly. Then quickly, suspiciously: "You ain't lyin' to me, are you? I ain't no cry-baby. I kin take it. Don't ever lie to me, Miss Nurse."

"I don't lie, Philip," Judith assured him. "It doesn't pay. Now I'm going to get you some warm milk and show you how easy it is to drink through a tube."

"I don't want nothin'," the boy protested. "It—it chokes me."

"This won't," Judith promised. "You'll see. We'll take it slowly and I bet you can do it. Why, I just bet you can do just about anything you want to. I'll be right back."

So together, Judith and Philip Conover began a fight for his life. Judith told Doctor Branch about the conversation the boy had overheard and protested against such thoughtlessness. How could anyone be sure the patient was completely comatose?

The resident agreed to take the matter up with the staff and see there was no recurrence. "But you realize, Morley," he explained in his forthright manner, "that the chances are all against the boy recovering the use of his legs even providing his heart holds out. Malnutrition—bad inheritance and poor environment have given him poor resistance. He was born with a heart condition that makes the job practically hopeless. It may be the chief will want to operate again a bit later; but I think it doubtful."

"Has Doctor Cranford given up all hope, Doctor Branch?" Judith asked, her heart sinking.

"Don't you know the chief never gives up hope, Morley?" the resident reminded her. "He'll cling to a thread —till it breaks."

"Then neither shall I give up hope," Judith said resolutely. "Just let me stay there in Pediatrics until Philip can wiggle his toes, Doctor. I have told him he is going to get well—he must, and I'm going to help him."

Doctor Branch patted her shoulder. "That's the spirit, Morley," he commended. "I'll see you remain where you are for a couple of months at least, unless——It'll take longer than that—but we'll see—we'll see."

"Thank you, Doctor Branch," Judith said and went back to the ward, her smiling face belying the ache in her heart.

During the days that followed Judith watched Philip Conover fail steadily. His stepmother worked in a canning factory in Wyckard, some dozen miles from Nottingham. There were four other children younger than Philip whom Mrs. Conover had been compelled, upon the disappearance of her husband, to put in a Children's Home.

"Men!" thought Judith bitterly. "What a lot of misery they cause!" And yet she felt sure that if the philandering Conover decided to return to his wife and family, the woman, would welcome him with open arms. Her lip curled in scorn. "How can women be so spineless?" she demanded of Brenda Newton after a visit from Phil's stepmother to the ward.

Brenda shrugged. " 'Love suffereth long and is kind,' " she quoted.

"Bosh!" Judith retorted and recalled how she had used that same quotation in describing friendship. "You are confusing friendship with love, Judy," Rufus had told her. How long ago that seemed! How could she have been so naive?

Back in her room next morning she found a note from Isabelle containing the news that "the Cranford-Booth nuptials" had been postponed. Judith turned the brief message over and over in her hand. What did that mean? Of course she had considered the whole thing sort of hurried; but just what had occurred to bring about a change of plans? She didn't know and told herself she didn't care either. She was tired and worried about Philip. She was staring out the window with unseeing eyes when she heard a knock on her door. She remained quiet. She wasn't in the mood for conversation. The knock was repeated—peremptorily.

"Come," she muttered inhospitably.

"Telephone, Miss Morley," the maid announced, her voice a mere whisper in deference to a possible sleeping nurse although it wasn't at all likely anyone was in bed this early.

"It's that same man," she went on, an interested gleam in her pale eyes.

"Tell him——Oh, never mind, I'll come down," she said, getting up from her chair and following the maid downstairs.

"I'm coming for you at one tomorrow, Judy," Rufus said without preamble. "I've something important to say to you. We'll go for a ride—come out here to the farm—or—well, we'll go somewhere. I must see you—alone."

"But Rufus——" Judith began.

"Listen, Judy. I must see you," he insisted.

"Oh, all right. But I ought not to go. I have a dozen things I should be doing tomorrow afternoon."

"Nothing is as important as what I have to say." Then he said: "Rain or shine, Judy. I'll be there. Good-bye."

Judith replaced the instrument with mixed feelings. Just what was it that was so important—that he had to tell her at once? She had been avoiding Rufus more or less successfully ever since the Easter dance. He had been to the house several times but she had pleaded business that permitted but a moment or two of her time for talk with him. Being on night duty had been some protection but there were her hours off—her twenty-four hour rest period when she had left word with the maid and Mrs. Martin, the house-mother, that she was not at home to anyone. Lately she had been slipping out for long solitary walks in the park. She felt she wanted to be alone. It seemed as if people bothered her—even her housemates got on her nerves. Isabelle insisted it was one of two things—love or night work. Rufus had threatened to do something about it.

"Don't you dare!" she had cried. "Please, Rufus. I'm

126

perfectly all right. It's just that I don't feel like gadding just now. I'm not good company, either. All my oomph and glamor, if any, have deserted me. Honestly, Rufus, I'm better by myself."

And Rufus had looked at her for a long searching moment and then gone away and Judith felt that he had read her soul. Had seen that she was pining for Larry Booth —that she was acting like a love-sick adolescent and her pride was in the dust. She hated him for prying. What business was it of his? Now what was it he wanted of her? All right. She would go out with him. She would listen to what he had to say. She would show the girls in the hospital and Larry Booth, too, that she didn't care a tinker's darn for him—that he could marry whom he pleased and it was nothing to her. She would show them.

She mounted the stairs with cheeks burning and eyes sparkling. Isabelle, who was now on night duty in Men's Surgical, came into her room followed by Brenda Newton. Isabelle stood off and surveyed the two with cynical eyes. "It's a toss-up between the pair of you," she said scornfully. "Snap out of it! Behold a brand new world outside. I tell you what you both need is a new heart interest. Nothing like it to pep a body up. Or failing that—a hat— one of the crazy things everyone is wearing this spring."

"Oh, keep still," Brenda begged. "Just because everything is on the up and up with you doesn't make you an authority on life, Isabelle Carey. All I need or want is to be let alone—given a decent amount of privacy. But do I get it? I do not. There's not a thing wrong with either Judy or me."

"No? Goody-goody!" Isabelle mocked. "Then let's all laugh and be gay. Sing for joy. Let's dance." She did a sprightly fandango, catching the smaller Brenda in a mad whirl about the none too large room. Judith laughed at Brenda's stubborn resistance. Brenda, who was naturally the very spirit of grace, was like a wooden image. At last, panting from her exertion, Isabelle sank into a chair. "I give up," she muttered, wiping imaginary sweat from her forehead. "You're even getting stiff in the joints. Stay out!" she commanded, in answer to a sharp knock on the door. Two nurses poked inquisitive heads into the room.

"What goes on here?" one of them wanted to know.

"Just pure animal spirits, Walker," Isabelle replied. "These two children are suffering from spring fever—or sudden reaction from too much night work, it's hard to tell which. Gosh! Me for my trundle, good people, and I advise you all to follow suit." She began to sing in her husky contralto:

" 'Sleep for the night is com-ing;
    Sleep through the sunny noon;
    Sleep while your pals are play-ing;
    Sleep—you'll wake all too soon.
    Sleep when you should be add-ing
    Millyun-buck-tan to your skin;
    Sleep for the night is com-ing
    When you must work like sin.' Ah-ah-ah-women!"

Judith watched the quartette go singing down the hall. She was smiling as she closed the door and prepared for bed. Isabelle was funny.

CHAPTER ELEVEN

ISABELLE CAREY knocked on Judith's door at four o'clock that afternoon. Judith was lying, hands behind her head, gray eyes fixed on the shadows cast on the wall of her room by the afternoon sun. She had been dreaming of Philip Conover. The dream was far from pleasant. Although she refused to acknowledge it even to herself. Judith knew the boy was dying. Her face was sad as she returned her friend's blithe greeting. As Brenda said, everything was on the up and up with Isabelle just now and her high spirits seemed to jar on Judith's sensitive nerves. The newcomer found a seat on the foot of Judith's bed and gazed anxiously at the girl before her.

"Don't you feel well, Judy?" she asked.

"Of course I feel well," Judith replied after a moment. "It's only that I dread going on duty tonight." Tears filled her eyes and she hastily winked them back.

"Why? Can't you plead illness—get a sub or something? What's up? Not the Conover boy——"

"Yes," Judith said. "He's dying and—I—I lied to him, Isabelle. I promised him he'd get well and strong and— wiggle his toes——" She turned over on her face and her shoulders shook with muffled sobs.

Isabelle was silent for a moment, her eyes tender. "I heard he couldn't possibly get well, Judy. I guess the chief knew from the very first it was touch and go with him. But listen to me, Judy. It won't do any good to give way like this. After all, the boy might better be dead than remain a helpless cripple all his life. As for your lying— it really wasn't lying, Judy. If you believe in another life then of course he'll be well and strong—'No more pain,' you know, and—he'll be able to wiggle his toes to his heart's content. What a thing to promise him! She said the last lightly.

Judith wiped her eyes. "You see, he was in a cast and I told him when he could wiggle his toes he would know the broken pieces were mending. He tried so hard to be patient. But his heart's bad, Isabelle—the poor youngster never had a chance from the day he was born, I guess. But he's been such a brick—has such courage—it's—it's tragic!"

"I know," the other agreed. "Now listen. Get into your gym togs and let's go downstairs——"

"No," Judith said. "I'm going for a walk—alone. I'll pull myself together quicker that way. I'm sorry," she added, at Isabelle's look of disappointment. "I'm no good just now."

"I wish I was sure the Conover boy was the real cause of your sudden loss of pep and—or what have you," Isabelle muttered, frowning.

Judith sat up in bed, her eyes suddenly dangerously bright. "What else?" she demanded. "You make me sick, Isabelle Carey. Just because you're in the throes of a death less love don't imagine everyone else has been inoculated with the same virus. And if you ever mention Larry Booth or Bernice Cranford to me again I'll—I'll—well, I'll never speak to you—I'll—I'll never forgive you. Now get out and let me dress."

"Wow!" Isabelle exclaimed as she stood up only to stare down at the flushed and angry girl on the bed. "Well, you needn't burst a blood vessel, darling," she soothed aggravatingly. "I was only doing a bit of psychoanalysis on the theory that to know oneself is to cure oneself. No hard feelings, I hope. Sorry I raised your blood pressure; but—well—see you at dinner and—I hope it won't be too tough on you tonight, Judy."

The door closed softly and Judith felt an urge to call her back. She was ashamed of her outburst. Isabelle hadn't meant to be mean. She got out of bed and slipped on her robe. A cold shower ought to clear her brain and put some energy into her listless body. It did. She dressed quickly and went down the back stairs and around the hospital to the street.

"When blue and out of sorts, buy a new hat," someone had said and this afternoon Judith went on a tour of the shops. She found a white felt with a tiny scarlet feather in its ribbon band and decided it was just what she wanted. A block farther on she located a plain white crepe sports dress with a red belt and red buttons marching down the entire front and bought that, too. Laden with her spoils she consulted her watch to find she must hurry back to the hospital. She felt better. After all, one had to have clothes even if one lived the life of a recluse—practically.

Suddenly she stopped in her tracks, the box containing the new hat slipping to the pavement. There was her date with Rufus Grant tomorrow afternoon. A wave of color flooded her face from chin to hairline. She picked up the hatbox and quickened her pace. Was it possible she had bought these things because she was going out with him? She certainly hadn't given the date one thought. It must have been her subconscious directing her steps and actions. What hooey!

She laughed softly to herself as she mounted the stairs to her room and changed into her uniform. Isabelle knocked on her door and when there was no immediate response, opened it a crack and tossed her cap inside. After a moment she entered, picked up the cap and pinned it on her head.

"I guess it's all right for me to come in. You didn't throw my cap out," she said tentatively, her eyes on Judith.

"Don't be silly," Judith smiled. "When have I ever kept you out—when has anyone for that matter—if and when you felt like entering? I'm sorry I blew up this afternoon, Isabelle. Look," she said as she opened the hotbox and lifted the new creation from its tissue paper. She removed her cap and put the hat on at a rakish angle. "Like it?"

"That's exactly the hat I want," the other girl exclaimed. "Where on earth did you get it?"

"Downtown—at Terese's. I got a dress, too."

"What's the occasion?" Isabelle wanted to know.

"Oh, I felt like splurging and—well—I splurged," Judith explained, her cheeks pink.

Isabelle eyed her quizzically for a moment but deciding discretion was the better part of valor, made no comment.

Judith replaced her cap and turned to face the other girl. She was smiling, although there was no mirth in her eyes. "Ready?" she asked. "It's lamb stew tonight, you know, and if there's one thing I detest above all others it's cold lamb stew. What say we pass it up, Isabelle? I'm not hungry tonight, anyway."

"You don't have to eat the stew if you don't want to," Isabelle said, slipping her arm through that of her friend. "I'm sticking to salads just now—watching my figger, you know. I peeped in at the kitchen before I came up here and, believe it or not, I saw strawberry shortcakes in a row on the counter by the pantry door. With real whipped cream too—or my eyes deceived me."

"You did!" Judith exclaimed. "Then what are we loitering for—let's go. But," she said as they rounded a corner in the corridor, "no doubt they're for the paying guests."

"You would think of that," Isabelle grumbled. "Why couldn't you at least have let me dream?"

But Judith's faked cheerfulness evaporated as she left the dining room and with Mary Olsen took the elevator to the children's ward. Clare Bruce's face was grave as they entered the long room. Amy Ingham shook her head at Judith's look of inquiry. So Philip was still alive. There was a screen around his bed. The other children seemed about as usual. If any one of them sensed the imminent approach of the dark angel, there was no evidence of it. Philip murmured continuously—sometimes unintelligibly. His thin face and glazing dark eyes tore at Judith's heart. He roused as Judith bent over him.

"Maybe — it's — most time — fer my toes — to wiggle, Nurse," he said gamely. "Do—do you—s'pose it is?" He paused to go on. "I—I—I feel—queer." His face was white and pinched. Judith consulted the chart and noted the ominous recording.

She soothed him as best she could, murmuring sympathy and encouragement. She was glad when Doctor Branch came into the ward. He looked grave as he joined her but smiled down at the boy whose eyes were fastened in agonized desperation on Judith's face.

"How goes it, lad?" he asked, his hand on the boy's pulse.

"Okay, Doc," Philip murmured. "Mebbe—I kin—kin wiggle—my toes to—morrow. Meb-be—that's why—I—I feel so—so funny."

"Where do you hurt, son?" the resident asked, nothing in his voice to show concern.

"Not—not hurt—queer—sort of——" His dark brows drew together and he closed his eyes.

"Well, well," Doctor Branch said. "We can't have that."

Philip's eyes opened for a moment and he watched the doctor and nurse narrowly. After the hypo he drowsed.

"Poor little chap," the doctor muttered.

Judith's eyes were full of tears as she slipped from behind the screen into the dim, sleeping ward. "How long, Doctor?" she asked.

"Not long," he replied. "His heart just couldn't take it. Don't cry, my child."

"He—he trusted me," Judith whispered. "I promised him he would be well and strong——"

"He will," the resident said quietly. "Somewhere in that other, fuller life he will be perfectly well and supremely happy. Maybe it's better—it must be. It's a tough world even for strong folks, my dear, and Philip would never have been strong if he were allowed to remain here. Death isn't the worst thing that could come to him—on the other hand I'm sure it is kind." He smiled at her as he patted her shoulder. "He'll soon be wiggling his toes, my child. That seemed the thing he wanted most to do."

Judith wiped her eyes and followed the resident to the door of the ward. "I wish I had known," she mourned.

"What could you have done more than you did?" the doctor asked. "You have made these few nights perhaps the happiest he has ever known. You have given him courage. He has been a brave lad."

"Will he suffer—will he——"

"We'll see that he doesn't," the doctor promised. "I'll be in again toward morning. He may not rouse. His pulse is very weak. Stay with him, my dear. If he wakens he will want you there. We'll get word to his stepmother in the morning. He died to her days ago. She is quite reconciled."

"How can she be?" Judith demanded stormily. "How can even a stepmother be reconciled to the death of a child?"

"And you, a nurse, ask that?" the doctor smiled. "You who have seen suffering and misery and want! How could she care for him? Supposing he lived, crippled, a helpless invalid all his days——"

"Oh, Doctor Branch," Judith cried, her throat thick with tears. "His father—why is he allowed to go scot free?" .

"Now you're getting into deep water, Morley," the doctor said crisply, running his fingers through his short upstanding white hair. "Some men are like that, you know. Philandering, irresponsible, lazy, shiftless. God knows why they are born and why they are permitted to marry and father the big broods they do. Don't worry your head about Pete Conover, my dear. He'll get his come-uppance. You know the old jingle.

" 'For every evil under the sun
There be a cure or there be none.
If there be a cure, then go and find it.
If there be none—why, never mind it.'

No cure has ever been found for philandering males—so let's never mind it."

Judith walked back to Philip's bed. He seemed scarcely to breathe. The dark lashes lay against his thin cheeks like smudges on alabaster. The pale lips were slightly parted. The brown hair looked limp and lifeless. She lifted a strand gently. It clung to her fingers. Tears slid down her face—she who was ashamed to weep—who was usually so poised and restrained. She was honest with herself. She knew her tears were not solely for Philip Conover. They were partly for herself; for the girl she had once been in that far-away Niles Corners. The girl in the makeshift graduating dress and too large satin slippers who had been the laughing-stock of her class. The girl who had gone into training at Procton, shy and lonely and ignorant of life and people, who had fought her way up to where she could be called "regular"—a worthy of friends such as Isabelle Carey and Brenda Newton and yes—Rufus Grant. The girl who for a few mad ecstatic months had believed —despite her fears and denials—that love was to be hers after all that Aunt Hepsie had said to the contrary—the love of Larry Booth. The girl who now felt betrayed and helpless.

The first call of a bird broke the quiet of the early morning. Three o'clock. A sigh came from the lips of the boy lying so white and still before her. The dark eyes opened for a moment and he smiled.

"It's time—Nurse," he whispered. Judith bent closer, her hand on his damp forehead. "I—feel—it in—my toes. To—morrow—I'll wig-gle 'em." The smile remained on his face, but the light went out of his eyes. Judith closed them, breathing a little prayer for his happiness in that other, fuller life.

"You look completely done in, Morley," Clare Bruce told Judith when she came on duty at seven. "I suppose Philip Conover died during the night? I thought he would," she went on as Judith nodded. "Well, it's a blessing. Poor kid. His stepmother will have one less mouth to feed."

Judith left the ward. She couldn't talk about it. She had grown to love Philip Conover. He seemed to fill a vacancy in her life. She ate little at breakfast and went directly to her room and to bed. She was physically and emotionally exhausted. Completely forgotten was her date with Rufus Grant.

A persistent knocking on her door roused her from the deep slumber into which she had plunged. Drowsily she

135

called "Come" and tried to orient her vagrant thoughts.

"That man is here—that Mr. Grant. He says you are expecting him."

"Wh-what?" Judith asked, sitting up in bed. "Expecting him? What time is it, Martha?"

"One o'clock, Miss Morley," the maid told her marveling that her favorite nurse failed to note the alarm clock on the stand beside the bed. Judith thrust her feet into mules and stood up.

"Oh, my goodness!" she exclaimed. "I forgot all about him. Tell him I'll be down in a jiffy, Martha. I'll hurry."

It wasn't much more than fifteen minutes later when Judith ran down the stairs and joined Rufus in the reception room where he stood at a window facing the court through which cars and trucks passed almost continuously.

Just now the ambulance had returned and stood before the wide receiving room door. Judith and he watched as the stretcher with its quiet burden was removed and taken inside.

"Please forgive me, Rufus," Judith apologized. "I overslept."

Rufus made a wry face.

"Apparently you were not as excited over this date as I have been," he told her. "But come on—let's go."

Judith wondered what cause there could possibly be for excitement. She stole a curious glance at the face of her escort as he turned the car and sped down the street to the main highway. His eyes were very bright but there were dark circles under them as if he had slept but little the night before.

"Where are we going?" she asked after they had left Nottingham behind them and were driving along the quiet country road leading to the Club. "To the Club? But I don't play tennis, Rufus, or golf either."

"Who said anything about tennis or golf?" he asked. "And we're not going to the Club. We're going to see an old lady who has been like a mother to me ever since my own mother died. She has a little place about five miles out this road—there, just beyond those hills off there. She is going to have a special luncheon for us and we're to have the place to ourselves for the afternoon because she always takes a long nap every day. Wait until you see it. It's a dream cottage."

"Lovely," Judith murmured and thought longingly of coffee and hot rolls and rest. She hadn't realized how weary she was. She should have sent word to Rufus that she was too tired to go out with him—that she was ill—dead. Anything that would have given her a few more hours of sleep.

Rufus glanced at her and snapped: "You're dead on your feet. Haven't they any sense in that place that they can't see you've been working yourself into a nervous breakdown? A fine hospital that takes no thought for its nurses! I'm going to do something about it. I know a couple of people on that board and I'll give them an earful——"

Judith was now wide awake. "Don't be so headstrong, my friend," she told him. "It isn't the work—I can stand any amount of work. I'm strong. But, you see, one of my children died early this morning. He fought so bravely —but——You see, I never gave him up—I thought that together we could pull through. Perhaps it is because I was tired—I don't know; but I suddenly felt drained—completely unnerved. Nurses should get used to losing patients; but somehow I never do, especially when it's a child."

"I'm glad you came out," Rufus said. "Do you realize I haven't had more than a glimpse of you in weeks? This afternoon we are going to rest and visit. Lean back and relax, Judy," he urged.

A peaceful quiet reigned while the powerful car slid along the smooth concrete highway. The hills were reached, circled, and Judith spoke.

"Tell me about the surprise you promised me. I adore surprises."

"I'm afraid this isn't the time for it," the man said

137

dubiously. "I guess you're not in the proper mood—too exhausted."

"Does it depend on my mood?" she asked. "I'm sorry, Rufus. Perhaps I should have suggested a 'rain check.' I'm not going to be very brilliant company this afternoon."

"Don't talk nonsense," he told her gruffly. "Who wants brilliant company? You're always charming in whatever mood. I'm glad you didn't put me off again. Well, here we are," as the car slipped through a gap in a flowering hedge and along a neat gravel drive to a low porch over which a rosebush in full bloom was trained. The house shone with fresh white paint. Flaming peonies bloomed in the borders; a round bed of geraniums and sweet alyssum centered the velvet lawn. A small, white-haired old lady came to the porch to welcome them.

"It's like a fairy tale," Judith marveled half aloud.

Rufus gave his hand to Judith and they went up the two shallow steps to the porch where the old lady stood with outstretched hands. Rufus kissed her familiarly and presented Judith. Mrs. Stuart took the girl's hands in both of hers while she looked at her through interested bright brown eyes.

"You're pretty, my dear," she said, smiling happily. "I'm glad. And you're good, too. My boy deserves the best. But come in, do. Rosie will be anxious to serve lunch. She fixed the chicken the way you like it, Rufus, and you must be sure to tell her it is perfect. I am very happy to have you both with me today, my dears," she went on, leading the way to the tiny parlor. "Do you want to freshen up a bit, Judith—such a right name for you, my dear. Names aren't always right, are they? The bathroom is down the hall—but you don't need freshening—you are like a flower. Dear me! I'm afraid I'm like all old people—I talk too much—just rattle on whenever I have someone to listen. Don't mind me. I'll see how Rosie is getting along."

"Isn't she a peach?" Rufus asked when their hostess had bustled away.

"She's darling!" Judith agreed. "Does she live here all alone? How does she manage?"

"Oh, Rosie is with her all the time and George—Rosie's husband—manages the place. He's a gentle giant and adores Mrs. Stuart. They have a small apartment upstairs. Oh, it was built on from the back so as not to spoil the appearance—Mom Stuart says." He laughed indulgently.

Rosie, a buxom, middle-aged woman in crisp blue percale, came to announce that luncheon was on the table in the dining room and urged that they come at once while things were hot. Mrs. Stuart met them at the door and escorted them to the daintily set table, a hand through an arm of each. She presided at the small table, chattering happily and urging them to eat heartily. Judith was hungry. Everything tasted extra good and Rufus, too, did full justice to the meal. At last they could eat no more and Rufus excused himself to pay his respects to Rosie in the kitchen. Judith half rose to follow. Mrs. Stuart nodded approvingly.

"She will be very pleased if you do, my dear," she said.

So Judith joined her praise to that of Rufus and Rosie beamed with pleasure. Mrs. Stuart pleaded weariness directly after lunch and went to her room. Rosie sang softly as she cleared the table and washed the dishes. It was all very peaceful and ideally homelike and Judith's tense nerves relaxed. She sank into a cretonne-covered Boston rocker with a feeling of utter contentment. Rufus settled himself opposite. Birds sang in the apple tree outside a window. From the distance came the sound of a dog barking—the lowing of cattle—the soft cooing of doves. Judith closed her eyes. How heavenly it all was! She was glad she had come. She had eaten too much—she couldn't seem to keep her eyes open.

How long she slept she didn't know. A sunbeam creeping westward entered the room and settled on her eyelids. Her lashes lifted. For a startled moment she didn't know where she was. Her wandering gaze met the smiling brown eyes of Rufus Grant.

"Oh, I'm sorry," Judith murmured. She looked at her watch.

"Merely forty winks," the man told her consolingly. "Feel better? You look almost rested."

"Oh, I am. Rufus, I'm ashamed. What must you think of me?"

The brown eyes glowed. "Do you really want to know, Judy?" he asked, leaning forward.

"I ate too much," the girl said hastily, something in the man's tones warning her. He must not.

Rufus left his seat and reached his hands to her, drawing her to her feet. "Let's get out. Let's walk about for a bit. I confess I ate rather greedily—I always do when I come here." They went outside, following the stepping-stone path to the little thicket behind which gurgled a tiny stream of clear, sparkling water. A bench faced a noisy, man-made waterfall and when Judith attempted to walk on, Rufus stopped her. "Let's sit here for a few minutes. I think I must tell you what I intended to, after all, Judy. I have thought of nothing else for days—and nights. I have to know, darling——"

"Oh, no!" Judith cried in alarm. "You must not."

"Why not?" he asked.

"Because——" she paused. She didn't know what he was going to say. It wasn't at all possible he was going to ask her to marry him. She bit her lip. What a fool she was!

"Listen, Judy. I love you. I want you to marry me. I have wanted to tell you this from the first time I saw you —the time you were so unkind to me. I know you can't love me right now—you're so sweet and lovely and good; but will you give me a chance to make you? Will you let me see you—often? Go out with me—be—be my girl?" he stammered boyishly, his eyes pleading.

"Oh, I wish you hadn't done this, Rufus," she said, slowly. "I can't love anyone. I can't marry anyone—ever."

"Nonsense!" Rufus declared emphatically. "Why not?"

Judith was silent for a long moment then her lips set

firmly and she turned to him. "I'm not of your world," she began, but he cut her short.

"That, again? What does position, wealth birth matter when two people love each other? I'm no great shakes as a matrimonial match if it comes to that. Don't be like that, Judy."

"But I am like it, Rufus," she said seriously. "Listen. My father left my mother before I was born. My name may not even be Morley. It was the name my mother claimed he used when she married him; but Aunt Hepsie who brought me up—with whom I lived"—she corrected —"professed to believe his name was not Morley—that he may even have had another wife. Oh, she made it very clear she thought Mother had been betrayed and deserted."

"And your mother?"

"Mother believed he had been robbed of everything he had, killed and buried somewhere in a nameless grave. There was no money to investigate. She went back to Aunt Hepsie's and I was born there months later. She was killed in an automobile accident while out with the man for whom she worked—a prominent insurance man. Aunt Hepsie instilled me with the idea that misfortune is the lot of all Leeds women. My mother was a Leeds—Alice Leeds. I never could believe my mother was bad—Aunt Hepsie and the neighbors insisted she was. But she was so lovely, Rufus —so gay—so wonderful to me. Her life with Aunt Hepsie was drab, sordid, unlovely without one redeeming ray of beauty or pleasure. She was young—her employer was kind to her. He was married with several children and gossip was unkind to them both. But I can't believe my lovely mother was anything but thoughtless and young. I was eight when she died. No one will ever know what my life became after my mother left me. Aunt Hepsie was a sick, bitter old woman. I went to school because the law demanded it; but I took care of her, the house and the garden until she died of a stroke the year I graduated from high school. Doctor Wales, who treated Aunt Hepsie, took me into his office and sponsored my entrance into Procton

Training School. But don't you see, Rufus, that I am not what I seem? That I can never accept love or marriage from any man?"

"Why, no," Rufus replied sturdily. "I don't see anything of the sort. What if your name isn't Morley? I want to give you mine, Judy. You're morbid, darling. Nothing in the past amounts to anything. We are living in the present —planning for the future. Don't you see, Judy? All that has gone before has only served to make you stronger— more appealing—dearer."

Judith shook her head. "You don't understand," she said sadly. "I am the last of the line, Rufus. The Leeds curse will die with me——"

"Rubbish!" Rufus declared robustly. "You're being melo- dramatic, girl. This is America—the twentieth century. It's what a man is that matters, not the accident of his birth— what his ancestors happened to be."

"You're wrong," Judith objected firmly. "We are what our ancestors made us. We can't deny our heritage, Rufus, and mine isn't good enough. Truly it isn't an inferiority complex—it's just that I know all about your family pride —the long line of famous men and splendid women who went into the making of Rufus Grant—that I refuse to listen to you. I know I'm right, Rufus, and some day you will thank me for saving you from making a ghastly mis- take."

"Listen, Judy. Is this the only reason you refuse to hear me? You don't dislike me?"

Judith smiled though her eyes were tragic. "Dislike you, Rufus? How could I? You're sweet. I like you much more than I want to——No, please!" as he caught her hands and attempted to draw her into his arms. "I can't listen to you. Don't you see, Rufus? I don't know what became of my father—what his name really is. He may be in prison ——Back in Niles Corners I'm an outcast—the child of a light woman——"

"Shut up!" Rufus cried and caught her fiercely in his arms. "You don't believe that and neither do I. You're

142

sweet—you're the girl I want for my wife—the mother of my children—and I mean to have you." His mouth found hers and for a long moment there was silence except for the noisy little stream that murmured and gurgled as it rushed and tumbled over the little dam. With a strangled cry, Judith tore herself free.

"Oh, why did you do that?" she gasped. "You've spoiled things. Now we can't even be friends and I need a friend——"

"I'm sorry, darling," the young man murmured; "but you're acting like the heroine in some Victorian novel, you know. Can't you see that it's you I want, not your ancestors —your Aunt Hepsie who was probably a warped, disappointed old maid——"

"She wasn't an old maid, Rufus," Judith said soberly. "Her husband left her for the wife of another man. You see?"

"He probably had cause if what you tell me about her is true—that is if she kept harping on the evils of men and the world in general. She certainly put her dark spell on you all right. But I intend breaking that spell. Certainly I'll be your friend if that's what you want—at present. But I give you fair warning here and now that I'll keep on courting you until you give in. Oh, of course not openly, you know,"—as Judith protested—"I'll not embarass you if that's what you're afraid of, you silly child; but I want you to understand that you're my girl. I want you to let that idea grow in your subconscious until the time comes when all this twaddle about the Leeds curse and bad heritage loses its grip on you."

The banter left his voice and he bent his head until his cheek rested upon her dark hair. "Trust me, darling," he murmured tenderly. "There isn't a power in the world that can come between us now that I know I have a chance— that it's not I but you departed Aunt Hepsie that keeps you from giving in. And between us we'll lay her ghost for good and all."

Judith drew a shuddering breath—almost a sob—and

143

for a brief moment rested quietly within the circle of his arms. But it was only for a moment, then she straightened. "We must go back to the hospital," she said in something of her old calm manner. "I'll say good-bye to Mrs Stuart and then we really must go." As he made no move to withdraw his arm she stood up, smoothing back her hair. "I'm serious about this, Rufus," she went on as he got quickly to his feet to stand beside her. "Please don't think things can ever be different between us. I appreciate your friendship more than you can ever know; but———"

Rufus smiled down into the lovely serious face raised to his. The gray eyes were dark with some intense inner emotion and he noticed how thin she had become. He caught her shoulders roughly and gave her a little shake. "Listen to me, Judith Morley. Don't tell me you're carrying a torch for Larry Booth———"

Judith stiffened and for a moment her face flamed then as suddenly whitened. The gray eyes blazed into his. "Doctor Booth is absolutely nothing to me," she said coldly. "I hope he and Bernice Cranford will be very happy. Now I must go, Rufus. Can't you see—can't you understand?" She pulled away from his restraining hand and hurried along the path to the cottage. Rufus watched her for a moment, his face troubled.

"Damn him for hurting her!" he muttered. "I'll make her forget him—I'll make her forget all the unhappiness and suffering she has had to endure. I'll make it all up to you, Judy, darling," he promised the vanishing girl and strode after her.

CHAPTER TWELVE

BRENDA NEWTON stood before the open window in Judith's room, her blue eyes blind to the glory of the June day. Her face was sad and her usually vibrant voice sounded flat as she discussed the advisability of going into Public Health work. She had a chance to go to New York for special training and thought she might take it.

"It'll be a change, at least," she said, turning as the door opened. Isabelle Carey entered. She stood for a moment, hands folded against her heart. her green eyes dark with excitement and happiness.

"Hank and I are getting married, girls," she announced without preamble. "This afternoon I maneuvered him into breaking down and popping the question and we're going to live in Beaumont in the very house I picked out. Ain't that som'pin', though? Gosh, I'm happy!"

The others hugged her, laughing at her excitement. The usually cynical Isabelle in the rôle of engaged girl was something new and delightful. Suddenly she startled them by bursting into tears. She wept stormily while Judith patted her back, murmuring soothing platitudes, and Brenda brought cold water and smelling salts.

"I'm a perfect idiot, girls," Isabelle gulped between sobs. "Can you feature me, hard-boiled, dignified Isabelle Carey, twenty-nine years old, weeping on anyone's bosom? It's— it's just that I thought he didn't want me—that I was going to lose him, and now when all the fear and dread are past, I'm a nervous wreck. If anyone had ever told me I'd be so sunk over any man I'd have slain them; but ——Oh, I'm ashamed of being such a weak sister; but I —I—I was all tied up in knots inside." She straightened, dabbed at her red-rimmed eyes and laughed shakily. "If you ever breathe a word of this to anyone, I'll—I'll put cyanide in your two-o'clock coffee. Oh, girls, I'm so happy!"

"Then, for Pete's sake, stop bawling," Brenda said shortly. "I never heard of such a thing." She swallowed once or twice before she went on—lightly, with natural curiosity. "Have you got a ring, Isabelle? Let's see it. When are you getting married?"

"Ring?" Isabelle asked, dazed. "Oh, you mean an engagement ring. I never thought of it. I don't suppose Hank did either. Gosh, girls, I wish I was off that Miller case. I'm dead on my feet—never slept a wink this morning worrying about our date this P. M."

"Going to tell Winters?" Judith asked.

"You bet your sweet life I am and how I'm going to enjoy that moment!" Isabelle said. "We are getting married on the very last day of June and you are both to come to my wedding—the only invited guests. Hank has nobody and the ones I have aren't enough interested in me to make the trip. Don't think I'm bitter about it. I'm too darned happy and thrilled to be bitter about anything."

"Well," Judith said slowly, "I hope you will be supremely happy, Isabelle, and I'm sure you will. Hank's a lucky man."

Isabelle left to change into uniform and Brenda, her eyes bleak, went to her own room. Suddenly Judith felt a pang of jealousy. Why couldn't it have been Judith Morley and—and——Her chin lifted. It could be. Rufus wanted her in spite of her background—in spite of her being other than what she seemed. Why should she mourn over Larry Booth's desertion? Rufus was worth a dozen of him.

At dinner that night, Isabelle drank several cups of black coffee. Her cheeks were bright with color and her eyes sparkled in spite of the dark shadows beneath them. Judith noticed the inquisitive glances turned toward her but Isabelle ignored them, chattering about everything except herself.

Judith was glad that she was going on day work in the surgical ward after her forty-eight hour rest period. Rufus wanted to show her his farm. She had put him off on every occasion he had invited her to make the twelve mile trip with him. She had gone many times that distance on other occasions but somehow she felt by going to the farm she

146

would be treading on dangerous ground . She told herself she was silly to feel that way and decided the very next time he asked her to go she would accept, let the regrets come later.

She had promised to go to the dance at swanky Appletree Inn out on the Turnpike although she shrank from contact with the engaged pair. She had heard rumors from others beside Isabelle, that the affair wasn't running smoothly. Bernice resented Larry's devotion to the hospital and had been seen on the bridle path with other men at different times—among them Rufus Grant.

Judith paid scant attention to this gossip. It was, of course, ridiculous. No girl formally engaged to Larry Booth would risk his anger and jealousy—risk a break. Larry was quick-tempered and possessive. He wouldn't stand for any two-timing. Judith was sure of that. After all, Rufus belonged to that crowd. He had been brought up with most of them. The fact that he owned and operated a farm some distance from town didn't keep him from taking an active part in the social life of Nottingham. After all, Andrew Grant, young Rufe's father, considered Nottingham his brother's home.

The dance was to be formal which meant she must have a new frock. Not that it mattered to her, she assured herself firmly. She had examined the maize chiffon she had worn at the Easter party and decided it wouldn't do. She wanted to be a credit to Rufus. She would ask Brenda to go shopping with her tomorrow afternoon. She preferred Isabelle's judgment on anything as important as this; but Isabelle was in the clouds. Brenda would have to do. She had good taste and was perfectly candid in expressing her opinions.

The dress proved a success from the moment Judith tried it on. It cost much more than she could afford but it did things to her gray eyes and dusky hair. She was glad her arms and shoulders were good and that the new hairdo was becoming. On the afternoon before the dance, she lay on her narrow bed, a pillow beneath her knees and her feet elevated in a position warranted to revive frayed nerves and stimulate the flow of blood to every part of the body. In other words, to provide pep, vigor and vitality to tired nurses. Brenda, on night duty in Receiving, lingered in the one easy chair the room afforded.

"You're luck to be off duty a couple of days after the dance, Judy," she offered. "I wish I were going." She bit her lip and stared straight ahead. The door opened to admit Isabelle.

"All ready for the big night, Judy?" she asked, standing tall and slim beside the bed. "I have news, my hearties. Bernice and Doc have had a fight—a terrific battle, so they say. Anyway, the wedding, that was to have taken place some time this month, has been postponed—until fall. I have my own opinion as to that. I bet the whole thing blows up."

Judith sat up with difficulty, kicking the pillow to the foot of her bed. "Don't be silly," she said coldly. "She's mad about him."

"Granted," Isabelle agreed, "and no doubt he's mad about her, too. But they're incompatible. I never thought it would work—that is, I had my doubts. It's business before pleasure with Larry and Bernice won't take a back seat for anyone or anything. I hear the chief has his hands full trying to keep the peace. He wants Doc as his assistant and for some vague and illogical reason he wants to keep his granddaughter in Nottingham. He's nuts, that guy. The gal's TNT."

Judith felt Brenda watching her. Did Brenda, too, think it made any difference to her what Bernice did or did not do or Larry Booth either? It was absolutely nothing to her. She managed a laugh at sorts and replaced the pillow beneath her knees before lying down again.

"The wiseacres tell us true love never did run smoothly," she said evenly. "No doubt it's just a passing storm. The air will be clearer afterward."

Isabelle stared down at her for a moment, grimaced and turned to Brenda. "Don't tell me you're not eating tonight either," she complained. "Just because Judy, here, happens to be going out in society and must look frail and undernourished, is no reason for the rest of us hard-working gals to follow suit. I confess she looks quite delectable but—let someone else do the devouring. How's Rufus, Judy?" she asked. "Seems to me you're showing signs of coming to your senses at last. Good work! Let's make it a double feature, darling. What do you say?"

Brenda's wide blue eyes examined Judith's serene gray ones for a sign of embarrassment but could find none. "Give me time, Isabelle," Judith told her inquisitor. "Don't rush me. After all, I've known him only since spring."

" 'Nor time nor space, nor deep nor high
    Can help my own away from me,' "

Isabelle quoted as she pulled Brenda to her feet and moved toward the door.

"Do you believe that, Isabelle?" Brenda asked, holding back for a last word with Judith.

"Sure, I believe it. Haven't I proof? Have a grand time, darling," she told Judith as she opened the door. "Come on, you dope," to Brenda. "All the best portions will be snatched and we'll get nothing but scraps. 'Bye, Judith. See you in the morning."

"Want me to bring you up a sandwich and a glass of milk?" Brenda asked solicitously.

"Not a thing," Judith told her. "I had a glass of milk and some crackers at four."

The door closed after the two nurses and Judith, prone on her narrow bed, tried to make her mind a blank—to quiet her racing pulses. What did it matter to her that Bernice and Larry were having difficulties? She hadn't seen Larry Booth to talk to in weeks. He had avoided her whenever possible. As for Bernice Cranford—Judith hated her wholeheartedly. And yet, she told herself, if it hadn't been Bernice, no doubt it would have been someone else. It just wasn't in the cards that Larry should belong to a nobody like Judith Morley. He was ambitious. Not only professionally but socially as well. But why couldn't it have been someone she could admire—like, even? She felt she would not have minded his defection so much in that case. She had an idea Liz Durnford was in love with him. She liked Liz and Liz had money and social position if not Bernice's amazing beauty. But what was beauty worth? It hadn't brought her happiness. It hadn't brought her mother happiness either. She felt the old feeling of fear and dread creeping over her. This would never do. She got to her feet and walked about the room. She wished tonight were over—she wished she wasn't going. She had half a mind to call Rufus and tell him she couldn't make it—that she was ill.

"Coward!" she accused her pale face as she caught a glimpse of it in her mirror. "Of course you'll go and you'll like it. You'll say 'yes' to Rufus if he asks you again—no—no—you can't. It wouldn't be fair to him." She buried her face in her trembling hands—her whole body shook with a nervous chill. She went to the bathroom and prepared a bromide, soundly berating herself for her weakness; for being scared to face Larry Booth and Bernice Cranford. Well, this summer she would apply for a position in some other hospital. Maybe she would go to New York or Philadelphia or Boston. Some big city where she could lose herself.

She dressed slowly and carefully. The reflection in her mirror heartened her. The bromide quieted the tumult in her blood and when Rufus arrived she was her old self, reserved, charming, even a bit provocative. That, she told herself, was the frock. Rufus took her two hands and swung them. He admired the gown, the new hairdo and the faint alluring scent that surrounded her.

"Gosh, Judy!" he exclaimed boyishly, "you're a knock-out!" He slipped her hand through his arm and hurried her out to the waiting car. Heads appeared in the windows and Judith waved. Rufus grinned up at them and they called greetings and goodbyes indiscriminately. Rufus was

150

popular with the nurses who thought Judith the world's prize idiot to allow him to remain in circulation. Not a girl there but would have jumped at the chance that Judith held so lightly. Judith wondered why she remained so unimpressed. She liked him—like him a lot. But love? No—no. She looked at the strong profile of the man beside her and told herself that if things were different—if her background were other than what it was, she would take a chance. She felt sure it wouldn't be hard to love Rufus. He was such a dear. Queer she hadn't thought it unfair to marry Larry if he were willing to take her as she was. She couldn't understand it.

They talked of many things on that twenty mile ride to Appletree Inn. No, Judith had never been here before. In fact she had been to few formal dances. Rufus seemed to sense her nervousness and turned to smile encouragement as she sat, her hands folded tightly in her lap, her eyes staring straight ahead.

"There'll be a lot of stuffed shirts there," he explained; "but they needn't bother us. You know the Staceys and Doctor and Mrs. Cranford and the Porters—Linus is staying in Arizona, by the way. What did you say?" he asked as Judith gasped at the news. So Mrs. Porter had maneuvered things the way she wanted them and Brenda was due for unhappiness. Rufus repeated the question.

"What's the matter?" he asked.

"Nothing. I was surprised that the Porters were back." That was a flat thing for her to say. The Porters were nothing to her—less than nothing. She scarcely knew them and she doubted if Mrs. Porter even remembered the nurse who had taken care of her husband during a tonsillectomy a year or more ago.

Rufus was looking at her inquiringly. Judith laughed. "One of my friends is a friend of the son—that's all. She will be disappointed that he isn't coming back."

"Anything serious?" Rufus asked idly.

"I hope not. She's too sweet a girl to be tied up with that family."

The man laughed. "Poor Linus has a mother complex," he said. "Your friend wouldn't have a happy time of it if she married him, my dear."

"I hope he marries a strong character," Judith said vindictively. "One who will inject some courage and self-assurance into him. He makes me sick."

"He won't," Rufus asserted positively. "He'll never marry anyone unless the girl kidnaps him. That might work. Your friend is lucky if she only knew it."

"I know," Judith retorted. "That's what everyone says when a marriage doesn't come off."

Rufus was silent for a long moment and Judith wondered if he thought she was speaking from experience. They turned in between stone pillars and drove along the winding road to the parking lot in the rear of the huge half-timbered mansion sprawling beneath giant elms and surrounded by velvet lawns and glowing flowers.

"Where are the apple trees?" Judith asked.

"The orchard is back—behind the stables and barns. It's quite an orchard at that. Some day we'll come out when it's daylight and wander about. It's really delightful. The cuisine is excellent, too, and I'm sure you'll like the orchestra and the floor."

"It's rather overwhelming," Judith whispered as she mounted the stairs beside him.

He laughed and patted her arm. "There you are," he said as they approached the dressing room before which stood a smiling maid in black satin and crisp white organdie. "I'll wait right here, darling," he whispered. "Don't be long."

The dressing room was crowded with laughing, chattering girls and women. Judith was surprised to find she no longer felt nervous. A maid took her light wrap and led the way to a mirror. Judith touched her hair and ran a puff over her nose. She smiled at the maid and went out into the hall. Rufus was waiting but he was talking to Larry Booth and Bernice Cranford. Bernice was standing close to him, one hand on his arm. Larry, who had always looked tall and distinguished in evening clothes, seemed almost small beside the other man. Bernice was laughing up at Rufus while Larry looked almost sulky. Judith's spirits lifted. She joined the three at the foot of the stairs.

"Hello!" she greeted Larry who stared at her in startled surprise. Bernice swung around and her face changed subtly.

"O-oh," she said impersonally, then—"Hello!" She still kept her hand on the black sleeve of the tall young man beside her who was smiling admiringly at Judith. Judith took a step nearer and Rufus held out his hand.

"Ready?" he asked and slipped her hand through his arm. Judith experienced a thrill of impish satisfaction at the blank look on Bernice Cranford's face. She knew both she and Larry were watching them as they mounted the stairs to the ballroom at the top of the house.

Young Rufe and Angela Stacy met them just inside the wide doors. Angela was on her best behaviour. She admired Julia's frock and exclaimed over her hair. Rufe informed his uncle that he intended having as many dances as he could with Judith and Angela did nothing more than wrinkle her lovely nose at him.

"I hate these affairs," Rufe complained. "No cutting in—if you get stuck with a droop why you just stay stuck for the duration. I tell you what, Unc. Let's have a closed corporation—let's keep our gals to ourselves. Turn about. What say?"

But Doctor Cranford came over and Judith promised him the first waltz. He had not forgotten the Easter dance. Judith felt she was a credit to Rufus—that he was even a little proud of her. She was glad. They had supper together—the four of them, and Angela became very friendly until Bernice Cranford and Doctor Booth drew chairs to their table and the talk became unpleasantly personal. Judith thought Bernice decidedly insulting to Larry and was disgusted that he showed no disposition to retaliate. Angela openly egged Bernice on, winking indiscriminately at everyone present. Bernice leaned across Judith to talk

153

to Rufus, then somewhat imperiously asked her to change places so she could carry on the conversation more comfortably.

"You and Larry can talk shop," she suggested cooly. "It seems to be what he's most interested in. I hope you don't mind, too much," she added as an afterthought.

Bernice slipped into the seat Judith vacated. Angela giggled and warned Rufus to watch his step. Liz Durnford had asked the same thing of Judith and she hadn't minded at all, or at least, very little. Now she was furious. Larry's face was a study. Rufus eyed Judith for a moment then appeared to accept the situation and bent his head to listen to Bernice Cranford's murmured confidences. Young Rufe grabbed Angela's hand and pulled her away from the table. Judith's glance followed them.

"They're a rowdy pair, arn't they?" Larry Booth said as the youngsters vanished. "That Stacy brat hasn't improved any since she was in the hospital."

"She's young and rather spoiled," Judith murmured, "but I like her."

The low-toned conversation continued at the other end of the table. How rude some af these wealthy girls were! Judith compared the girl beside her with the nurses in the hospital and wondered how Larry Booth could have chosen her when there were so many finer girls so close at hand. To be sure she had beauty and social standing but she was arrogant, rude and ill-tempered. How could Rufus sit there and listen to her—how could he have been willing to have her give up her seat to Bernice Cranford; for he was willing—maybe even eager? The girl's eyes never left his face. Judith tried to close her ears to that low murmur which appeared to be confined almost entirely to Bernice. What was she saying?

An inn attendant hurried over to the table. He appeared excited and stooped to whisper in Doctor Booth's ear. "Are you Doctor Booth?" he asked.

Larry nodded and rose to his feet. The attendant's voice was almost inaudible.

"There's been an accident a mile or so up the road. Doctor Cranford sent me for you. He said there was a nurse here, too."

Larry held out his hand. Judith stood up. "I'm a nurse," she said simply.

"Will you come? At once?"

Larry looked at Bernice who had turned and was staring at him defiantly. Rufus took a step toward Judith. Bernice put a restraining hand on his arm. His brown eyes met Judith's briefly and she murmured regrets at leaving. He said nothing.

"If you go now, Larry Booth, you needn't come back— ever," Bernice said, her voice low and menacing.

"It's an emergency, darling," Larry told her. "What else can I do?"

"An emergency—it's always an emergency. Oh, go— go and stay. You heard me. I warned you. I'm sick of it. Go on—you two. Rufus will take me home."

The attendant warned them to silence. The dance must not be spoiled. He turned away. Larry and Judith followed. Larry waited while she hurried to the dressing room where she took the wrap the maid handed her and together they sped down the stairs to the lower hall. Doctor Cranford had gone on ahead. It was the first time Judith had been in Larry's new car. He had bought it after the advent of Bernice. She gave a brief passing regret for the lovely frock she was wearing but banished it before the graver business at hand.

The whole incident had taken but a few minutes and they reached the scene of the accident almost before Judith had time to wonder much about it. Of the three machines involved in the accident, only the truck remained upright. The cars were a total loss. Two ominously still figures lay on the grass beside the highway, the moonlight showing with horrid clarity their wide open eyes and battered bodies. Doctor Cranford was working over a child who was moaning piteously. A woman sat leaning against one of the trees that lined the road. She was bleeding from a

155

cut on her head but made no sound. A man shrieked in agony and Larry Booth went directly to where he lay, pulling Judith along with him. The child's moaning became a whisper and was still. The woman toppled over and lay quiet in the grass. Doctor Cranford carried the child to his car. He returned to kneel beside the woman. The shriek of the ambulance siren as it approached the spot roused the truck driver. Up until then he seemed stunned. A car came to a stop beside the truck. Two troopers got out. The man and woman who were still alive were lifted into the ambulance. Doctor Cranford followed it back to Nottingham in his car. Out of the night other cars appeared. The coroner and undertaker came. The bodies of the dead were removed. One trooper drove the truck away—the others remained, directing traffic, urging on the morbidly curious, protecting the scattered belongings of the victims. Judith answered questions automatically—she felt numb.

"Let's get out of here," Doctor Booth said at last. "We've done all we can. Want to go back to the Inn, Judy?"

"Like this?" Her dress was torn and stained with blood. Her hair was disheveled and she was achingly tired.

"I suppose not. I don't imagine it would be any use anyway. We'll go back to the hospital."

They passed the Inn ablaze with light. The clock on the instrument panel said 1:45. Larry drove silently for some ten or twelve miles.

"I've been a damned fool," he muttered as if to himself.

Judith said nothing. At the nurses' home she climbed the stairs to her room one step at a time, like an old woman. Every one of the two hundred six bones in her body ached, every nerve shrieked from weariness. She slipped out of her clothes and flung herself into bed and knew nothing more until noon when Isabelle and Brenda crept in to stand aghast at the ruin of the exquisite frock.

"What on earth happened, Judy?" Isabelle asked pointing to the torn and stained heap on the floor. "Accident? Were you hurt?"

"Not I," Judith said shudderingly, still slightly sick from the experience. "A truck and two cars crashed about a mile from the Inn. The chief called Doctor Booth and me to help. It was awful!"

"What a rotten shame!" Isabelle cried. "Did they bring them here to Nottingham?"

"Three of them. A woman, a man and a child. Two men were killed. I don't know what became of the truck driver. The troopers took charge of him. He looked drunk to me; but of course it might have been shock. He had nothing to say—just acted dumb." She shuddered again.

"Your lovely dress," mourned Brenda. "You ought to make the chief buy you a new one. After all, you were off duty. They make me sick here. We're supposed to have no life of our own at all. We belong to the hospital, body and soul. Why do you stick, Judy?"

Isabelle came over to the bed and felt Judith's head. "No fever," she pronounced. "Want to sleep some more? Want us to get out and leave you alone? Of course we're dying to hear all about the dance; but maybe some other time, eh, what?"

"Some other time, please," Judith begged. "I'm completely shot. Too much night work I guess and then this. Oh, we lead a merry life, we nurses!" she finished wryly.

"I'll bring you up something to eat—coffee and toast, maybe, or some fruit juice," Brenda offered.

"No, don't," Judith said, shaking her head. "Just leave me alone for a little while. I'll be all right. I'm not hungry, anyway. I'll see you later."

Isabelle paused when she reached the door. "I hate to break bad news while you're sunk, Judy; but you're posted for night work in Men's Surgical—beginning at seven tonight."

"Oh, no!" Judith cried. "I have tonight off—my forty-eight hours' rest period——"

"I know, honey," Isabelle interrupted, "but it seems this is an emergency of some sort and you're drafted. No doubt you'll be given that extra time later."

157

"I bet she won't," Brenda said. "Promises—that's about all we get here. This hospital owes me a month already—counting all the extra hours I've put in. I'm getting out. I don't think I like private hospitals. Never again! Oh, come on, Isabelle. Let Judy rest. She certainly needs it. See you at dinner, darling."

The girls left and Judith lay and reviewed the events of the night before. Rufus had made no effort to detain her when Doctor Cranford sent for her. He hadn't even said good-bye or been interested in her leaving. Why was that? Was he, too, hypnotized by the blonde beauty of Bernice Cranford? Were he and Larry Booth rivals? Was he merely using her to bring Bernice to him? In her heart she didn't believe it; but she was sore and more than a little surprised that he had not followed her. She wondered what Bernice told him. Whatever it was he seemed intensely interested.

Judith lay with closed eyes seeing again the lovely face of the chief's granddaughter turned towards Rufus, her blue eyes with their long curling lashes never once leaving his. What had Larry meant by saying "I've been a fool? A fool to put his work first—before Bernice? Or a fool to aspire to her at all? And why did Bernice treat him so summarily? Was it possible she had tired of him already? Not at all likely. Perhaps she saw in Rufus Grant a chance to discipline her fiancé. It wasn't possible she was in love with Rufus—or was it? Oh, no! Judith wasn't aware that she spoke aloud. She slipped into her mules, caught up her robe and went down the hall to the showers. Nothing was to be gained by conjectures. Anyway, it couldn't matter to her. But suddenly she knew that it did.

CHAPTER THIRTEEN

RUFUS CAME THE nurses' home late on that same afternoon. He looked as if he hadn't slept. Judith met him in the reception room where a group of nurses were entertaining friends. All conversation ceased when Judith entered. She greeted Rufus as if nothing had happened and he said:

"I have the car. Come on out for a while. There are things I've got to know."

For a moment Judith thought of refusing. She was still hurt and angry and felt she wanted nothing more to do with him or any man. But noting the interested glances cast in their direction, she thought better of it.

"All right," she agreed. "I'll get a hat."

Nothing was said until they were out of the city. Rufus reduced speed and turned to a side road where traffic was practically nil.

"Now then," he said, parking in the shade of a huge maple tree, "I want to get things straight—or I can't go on."

"Go on?" questioned Judith. "Go on where?"

"Trying to make you forget Booth—trying to make you aware of me."

Judith stiffened. "Doctor Booth is nothing to me, Rufus. You insult me when you intimate he is."

"Is that the truth, Judy? I have to know."

"Well you know now," Judith said coldly. "I have told you before. Why this sudden doubt?"

"You were eager enough to go with him last night when he crooked his finger to you," he reminded her angrily.

"Doctor Cranford sent for me. You know that. There was a bad accident but you know that, too," Judith told him with anger matching his own.

"No, I didn't know it. How could I? No one told me. Anyway, you were not on duty last night. You were my guest——"

"Oh!" Judith interrupted icily. "You remember that? It looked very much to me as if you had forgotten."

Rufus turned and pulled her roughly against him. "Bernice is jealous as the devil of you. Why?" he demanded.

Judith stared at him with eyes that darkened in dismay. "Jealous of me? Oh, she can't be. Larry is mad about her——"

"It didn't look like it last night," Rufus muttered, relaxing his hold and staring straight before him. "He wanted her to change seats with you——"

"Don't be an idiot, Rufus," Judith said, her spirits suddenly lifting. "He had nothing to do with it. You heard Bernice ask me to change places. Doctor Booth and I didn't exchange a dozen words then or afterward. Two men were killed, Rufus, and three other people were injured—one a child. It was awful!" She pressed her hand to her eyes as if trying to shut out the sight of those bruised and broken bodies. Would she ever get used to these things? "After the ambulance came we went back to the hospital. Then I went home and straight to bed. I suppose Doctor Booth did likewise. It was a ghastly accident. Even doctors and nurses have feelings, you know, although we're not supposed to. Coming on top of everything it just about finished me. I ought not to have gone to the dance in the first place. I was too tired. I'm sorry if you misunderstood, Rufus; but you must remember I'm first of all a nurse."

"Nonsense!" he protested, still moody. "You're first of all a woman." He stared silently at nothing for a long moment while Judith watched him with growing excitement. Suddenly he turned. "Will it make any difference to you to know that Bernice has broken her engagement to Doctor Booth—definitely?"

Judith's heart leaped, then sank. She felt the man's eyes on her face and forced herself to speak quietly. "Why won't you believe me, Rufus?" she asked earnestly. "I tell you it makes no difference at all to me. Larry Booth is absolutely nothing to me. What is more, he never could be. I doubt if he ever was. Bernice Cranford has nothing to do with it. Anyway, what difference does it make to anyone?"

He seemed not to have heard her question. "Bernice told me she was breaking her engagement because she had discovered that you two loved each other. Why——"

"Don't ask me why Bernice Cranford or anyone should make such a statement," Judith interrupted sharply. "She undoubtedly has some plan in mind. Do you know, Rufus, I ought to be very angry with you for persisting in this; but somehow I can't. It all seems so perfectly silly. Anway, you know why I shall never marry. I told you." She said it sadly but firmly. "Now let us change the subject. Please don't refer to it again."

Rufus gave a prodigious sigh. "Maybe you think I'm a presumptuous fool, Judy," he said; but I—well, I told Bernice that you—that I—well, I said you and I cared for each other and that Larry Booth hadn't a prayer."

"You did?" Judith exclaimed. "Why on earth did you say that? I told you——"

"Oh, that!" Rufus scoffed.

"Yes, that," Judith repeated. "Even if I loved you with all my heart I still wouldn't marry you, Rufus. How could I? How do I know what my father is—where he is—whether my name is Morley or Leeds or if I'm nameless. I tell you, it wouldn't do at all."

"Use your head, girl," the man said impatiently. "Take a good look at yourself in the glass sometime. Can you doubt that your blood is pure—your parentage above reproach? I don't care what your Uncle Jeremiah told you——"

Judith laughed hysterically. "It was Aunt Hespie, darling."

"Well, Aunt Hespie, then. She had probably soured on life. She was no doubt a sadist. You say yourself that your mother was sweet and lovely. She told you your father was big and handsome and wonderful. Why not take her word for it? You're morbid, girl. When will you marry me, honey?"

"Oh, Rufus!" Judith cried. "Why do you persist in making it so hard for me? I do care for you—more than any man I know and if things were different—if I could be sure about my father—about oh, so many things—perhaps I could even love you——But I can never marry you. It wouldn't be right to you. Some day you would blame me for it and I—I couldn't bear it. We're getting nowhere."

"Listen, Judy. I'm not going to keep pestering you. if, as you say, it makes you unhappy. But I'm going to stick around—if only to keep other men away, and some day you're going to feel sorry for me and marry me—perhaps just to put me out of my misery. For that time, I'm willing to wait. I think you're wrong-headed and morbid and supersensitive; but I love every hair on your lovely head, Judith Morley, and don't you ever forget it." He caught her to him and kissed her hard and for a moment her lips responded.

"You're such a darling, Rufus!" she murmured as she drew back from his embrace. "But don't think I shall ever change—I can't. I've got to be strong——"

"Never is a long time, Judy, and I have all the rest of my life to convince you. I'm starting right now. Where shall we go?"

"I have little more than an hour. Let's just ride around for a bit, shall we?" It is lovely out this way—so quiet and peaceful."

"When do you have a whole day off? I mean twenty-four hours," he asked after a moment.

Judith shrugged. "By rights I should have tomorrow off besides tonight; but I have been informed by the powers that be there exists an emergency in Men's Surgical and Judith Morley must forego her rest period and report for duty at seven tonight. I have not the least idea how long the emergency will last; but I certainly hope it won't last long. I'm tired."

"I know you are," Rufus said. "Well, the very next time you have twenty-four hours off duty, we're going out to the farm. I want to show it to you, Judy. You'll love it. I'll call you every afternoon at two or so and you must keep me posted. Understand? I think I shall be masterful in the future—maybe I'll get further."

Judith laughed. "Cave man stuff, eh? It might work with some girls, Rufus; but I don't think I'm the type."

"We'll see," the man told her. "Sometimes these independent girls find they like being bossed—makes them feel protected and cared for."

"That would be something entirely new to me, Rufus," Judith told him seriously. "You know some people are born independent, some acquire it, and others have it thrust upon them willy-nilly. I belong to the last group. Maybe at heart I'm a clinging vine—a shrinking violet. Sometimes I have a longing to belong to a family—bury my head in my mother's lap and simply bawl my heart out."

"You poor kid!" Rufus said softly. "I've felt much the same —at times. Even men get spells of loneliness, you know. I lost both parents in a plane crash when I was in Prep School. Like you, I've had to solve my problems by myself in my own way. My brother had his own life— his own family problems to face. I couldn't dump mine in his lap, too. Well, darling, you're not alone any longer— you've got me, you know. My shoulders are ready to take over all your difficulties. They're broad and you have my permission to weep on either of them whenever you feel the urge. But after we're married, my dear, you'll never have cause for tears. I'll take care of that."

Judith laid her hand on his for a moment. "You're sweet, Rufus," she said softly. "I wish——"

A car rushed toward them, slowed and passed. Rufus swore under his breath.

"Blasted fool!" he muttered. "Is he blind or drunk? He's stopping—no, he's going on—driving as if the devil himself was after him."

Judith recognized the car. It was Doctor Booth's. What

163

ailed him? He didn't usually drive at that pace. Perhaps something was the matter—an accident somewhere.

"Let's go back, Rufus," she said impulsively. "There are things I must do and anyway it's nearly dinner time. You've been so kind to me—I feel rested."

"The hour isn't nearly up, Judy," Rufus protested, but he started the car and turned obediently. He drove slowly and as he drew up at the curb in front of the nurses' home, he reminded her that he expected to have her next free day. Judith promised and left him.

Upstairs in her room she changed quickly into uniform. The house was quiet—unnaturally so it seemed to her. She went down the hall to Isabelle Carey's room. It was empty. So was Branda Newton's. Downstairs she encountered no one and went to the gymnasium. It was five-thirty. Surely the girls couldn't be down here still. The big room was empty. Where was everyone? She went back to her room to find Isabelle and Brenda sitting calmly on her window-seat, a basket of cherries between them.

"Where on earth have you been?" Judith asked "I've looked everywhere for you. How long have you been here?"

"Just a few minutes. We went out to buy these. Have some," Isabelle offered.

"What's up?" Judith asked. "Is anything the matter here?"

"Nothing more than usual," Brenda replied. "Why?" Judith hesitated.

"Well?" Isabelle prodded. "Out with it. Give."

"Rufus and I were out in the country and Doctor Booth passed us driving like mad. I thought something terrible must have happened."

"And you ditched Rufus and hurried back to pick up the pieces, I suppose," Isabelle said cynically. "Always the conscientious nurse—Nightingale incarnate. You make me sick, Judy Morley. Can't you ever forget this darned place even when you're off duty?"

"I guess not, Isabelle," Judith muttered morosely.

"That's why I'm getting out," Brenda said, throwing a handful of cherry pits into the basket.

"Well, before you quit, you can just empty that basket. Brenda Newton," Judith told her crossly. "I hate garbage lying about in my room, and you know it."

"Okay," Brenda murmured, her mouth full of fruit. "I intended doing that little thing, darling. Oh, I almost forgot. A long-distance telephone call came for you just a little while ago."

"For me?" Judith's heart sank. Maybe Mrs. Leeds was dead or dying. "Was I supposed to call back?"

"I don't know. Martha took the message. I thought she left a note here for you. She said she was going to. I don't see it anywhere. Run down to the kitchen and ask her about it, why don't you?"

Judith found Martha at the telephone in the lower hall. She held out the instrument as Judith appeared.

"It's for you," she said.

Judith's face became grave as she listened. Mrs. Leeds was dying. She wanted to see Judith. Could she come at once? Judith told the nurse at the other end of the line that she would try. She replaced the telephone and went directly to interview the superintendent with but little hope of success. She felt, however, that she must go. Mrs. Leeds had been so wonderful to her. She owed her a tremendous debt.

Just as she feared, the superintendent refused permission and Judith hesitated for barely a moment before she said firmly:

"It is imperative that I leave at once, Miss Winters. Mrs. Leeds is dying. She has expressed a wish to see me. I must go."

The superintendent's eyes became glassy with anger. "Don't use that tone to me, Morley," she said icily. "You have obligations here——"

"And what's all this?" The resident had once again come to the rescue. Now he stood quietly beside Judith in front of the superintendent's mahogany desk.

165

"Nothing that I can't handle, Doctor," Miss Winters said coldly.

Judith turned away, her face white with anger. She reached the door and turned to face the room. "My dearest friend and adopted grandmother is dying. She sent for me. I want to leave—I am leaving—at once," she ended defiantly.

"You can't——"

"Of course you must go," Doctor Branch said crisply. "What ails you, Julia?" he asked, turning to the superintendent who had half risen from her chair. "Run along, Morley. I'll take the responsibility. Miss Winters just didn't understand the situation—did you Julia?" he asked, glaring at the irate woman who had dropped back and gave him glare for glare.

Judith fled, but not before she heard the resident repeat the warning he had given Miss Winters once before. "You're hanging yourself, Julia Winters. This can't last much longer. Didn't hear Doctor Branch say: "You'll have mutiny on your hands first thing you know and then what'll you do? Morley's one of our best nurses——"

"Best nurses indeed," Winters sniffed. "Gallivanting all over creation with Doctor Booth——"

"Nonsense!" interrupted the resident. "Doctor Booth's engaged to the chief's granddaughter."

"That's what you think. I happen to know the engagement's off. 'Our best nurse' as you call her is responsible——"

"You're dreaming, Julia. Who told you all this?"

"Miss Cranford told me—confidentially. It seems Doctor Booth became involved with Morley long before Bernice came to Nottingham and when he fell in love—apparently in love," she qualified, "with Bernice. Morley began making trouble between them with the result that Bernice broke her engagement. Of course Bernice is heartbroken but she feels that Doctor Booth's loyalties belong to Morley. That's the whole story and don't you dare breathe a word of it to anyone. I think we should let Morley go."

Doctor Branch thrust his fingers through his upstanding white hair then threw back his head and laughed robustly. "What a gullible female you are, Julia," he said. "I could point out a dozen holes in that wild tale, my dear. Do you mean to tell me, intelligent woman that you are, that you haven't seen what's been going on right beneath your eyes? Why, Bernice Cranford had no intention of marrying Larry Booth—not from the first. She took him on for a while to be sure—but when he had served his purpose she brushed him off, as the youngsters say so descriptively. Judith Morley isn't interested in him—I doubt if she ever was. Rufus Grant had been courting her for months. That's where the shoe pinches, my dear blind woman. Bernice wants Rufus. He's a better match."

"You're an old gossip, Amos Branch," the superintendent snapped. "I don't believe a word of it."

"You don't have to. Just wait and see. But listen to me, Julia Winters, if you don't watch out, you'll be the one to go. I could tell you some things that would make you a little more careful, but I don't think I shall. Maybe it would be a good thing for Cranford Memorial if we had a new superintendent. You make me sick." He walked to the door, paused and came back to stand beside the desk. "I warned you before and I do it again for the last time. Come down off your high horse, Julia, my girl. Stop playing dictator and mix a little of the milk of human kindness into your treatment of the nursing staff. The idea of refusing to let Judy Morley go to the sickbed of her grandmother! It's inhuman, that's what it is, and you can't get away with it."

"Mrs. Leeds isn't her grandmother. Morley has no relatives at all. I don't know how she ever was admitted to the staff in the first place. From what I hear, she has no background whatever——"

"Now who's an old gossip?" the resident wanted to know. "Judy Morley's a lady. That's more than can be said of some folks I know."

"Get out of here, Amos Branch," the superintendent

ordered, furiously, getting to her feet to stand menacingly before him. "You're insulting——"

"Oh, go jump in the lake," the resident retorted disgustedly. "I guess I'll just have to let you cut your own throat. I've done the best I can for you—now you can go your own gait. I'm through."

He went out banging the door behind him. It wasn't a door that banged easily and Miss Winters slumped into her chair, trembling with rage and something else. Was it fear? Was it true there was dissatisfaction with her management of the staff? She would ask the chief. He was an old softy —she could get around him easily. Doctor Booth didn't like her and if he was given the post of assistant surgeon in the fall, she supposed she might as well resign. Tears of anger and self-pity filled her eyes. She had given the best years of her life to this hospital. They couldn't let her go. She wished she hadn't been so arbitrary in her treatment of Morley. Morley was a good nurse—popular and docile. Perhaps Amos was right. Maybe Bernice was jealous of Morley though why she should be was inexplicable. Bernice was very beautiful—why, she could get any man she wanted. She knew she had been flattered at the girl's confidences—had been properly incensed at Morley's perfidy, promising to take drastic steps. Now she wasn't so sure. It was news to her that Rufus Grant was paying court to Judith Morley. How did Amos know so much? That's it, the nurses adored Amos. They told him things—intimate, personal things.

She tapped the blotter on her desk with nervous fingers. Perhaps it wasn't too late to do something about it. If she played her cards right, even now, it might be Amos who was let out instead of her.

CHAPTER FOURTEEN

JUDITH REACHED the Leeds summer home at a little before midnight. Mrs. Leeds was still alive and Judith was taken directly to her room. The girl was shocked at the change in her friend. But in spite of her bodily weakness her spirit flared, vivid and eager, as it had on the night of their first meeting.

"I'm glad you have come, my dear," she said as she held Judith's hand in both of hers. "Sit here beside me. Tell me what you have been doing—the good times you have had—the friends you have made—the people you have nursed. I want to hear it all—and the time is getting short. Do you mind, Judith? Are you too tired?"

"No," Judith assured her, trying to make her voice bright and free from sorrow. "I'm not a bit tired. I've been work·ing hard, darling. The hospital has been crowded all the time. One of my best friends is getting married this month —to a doctor——"

"And you? Are you in love yet?" The old eyes searched her face and Judith felt herself blushing although she shook her head vigorously. "I think you are, my dear," Mrs. Leeds went on softly. "Tell me about him. Is he good? Is he worthy of you? I wish I could see him. I wish you had brought him with you. What's his name?"

And suddenly Judith felt impelled to tell her about Rufus Grant. She knew it would make her friend happy to feel she had at last met a man whom she could love, and just now she felt that she loved Rufus with all her heart. She began with the telephone message, making it as amusing as she could. Mrs. Leeds smiled from time to time as the story grew and her hand pressed Judith's in sympathy.

"Do you suppose he would come up here if you asked him, Judith?" she asked when the girl finished her recital by saying:

"That's all, darling. We're not engaged—yet."

"Will you telephone him, Judith—in the morning? Ask

him to grant the last wish of an old woman who loves you. I can tell when I see him whether he is worthy of you—whether I can give you my blessing."

"But—we are not engaged——" Judith began again.

"You are afraid, my child. Afraid of love. Afraid to be happy—to follow your heart," Mrs. Leeds said softly, her dimming eyes on the girl's downcast face. "Don't ever refuse happiness, Judith. It is a priceless gift—grasp it with both hands—guard it with your life—nourish it and be grateful——"

"I will call him in the morning," Judith promised, noting the ominous shadow on the woman's face. What did it matter that she must cling to her determination not to marry anyone? Rufus would understand. She could explain everything to him.

But as it happened she didn't call Rufus in the morning. There was no need; for at three o'clock Mrs. Leeds died—quietly and peacefully, her hand still in Judith's, a smile of serenity on her face. Judith sent a wire to Doctor Branch. She would remain until after the funeral.

The hospital seemed very far away—completely outside her orbit of living. She wondered idly if she even had a job and somehow didn't seem to care. Mrs. Leeds was gone—leaving a void that nothing could fill. The funeral was simple, but crowds lined the road leading to the cemetery and surrounded the newly dug grave.

Back in the house, strangely empty now, Judith was preparing to return to Nottingham when she was summoned to the library to listen to the reading of the will. She wondered why she was there in the pleasant book-lined room; but found a seat with the two nurses and servants. They were all there—everyone in Mrs. Leeds' employ. She listened absently. There was a long list of bequests and near the end she heard her own name mentioned.

"To my dear granddaughter-in-love, Judith Morley,
I give the sum of five thousand dollars, tax free."

Judith sat for a long moment after the lawyer's sing-song voice had ceased. The servants were frankly weeping and the two nurses, who for years had been Mrs. Leeds' almost constant companions, stared at each other in wonder. No further need for either one to work another day if she didn't want to. Mrs. Leeds had remembered every one of those in any was associated with her. Her beloved home on the lake was to become a retreat for convalescents under the supervision of Doctor and Mrs. Horner—friends of long standing.

Judith was summoned to the superintendent's office next morning after chapel, expecting to hear herself summarily dismissed. Instead, Miss Winters expressed regret for the misunderstanding that had occurred on the occasion of Judith's request for leave of absence and suggested she take forty-eight hours off duty in order to recover from the distressing experience through which she had passed. Judith was too surprised to do more than murmur a stereotyped "Thank you, Miss Winters," and hurry back to her room where she flung herself across her bed to stare at the ceiling trying to solve the mystery of the superintendent's sudden change of front.

"Bless you, Doctor Branch," she said aloud at last. "You're a lamb. But at that, I almost wish she had dismissed me. It would have been a way out. And yet why should I want an out?" Suddenly the memory of that legacy returned to her. Why, she was rich! It was more money than she had ever had in her life or hoped to have all at one time. To some people it might not appear wealth; but to Judith Morley it meant safety—security—freedom from the haunting fear of poverty. She turned over on her face and wept a little for her friend. She would miss her. It had meant so much just knowing she was alive—on the same planet.

"Don't every refuse happiness, Judith," Mrs. Leeds had said. "It is a priceless gift—grasp it with both hands—guard it with your life—nourish it and be grateful."

She wept again, this time for Judith Morley—the girl who was a coward. No. She would not be a coward. She was entitled to happiness—everyone was—if they could get it. She lived over again those last hours with the dying woman—lived again the telling of the story of Rufus Grant's wooing. A warm flush crept to her hairline and she sat up abruptly. She would call Rufus and tell him she was to have two whole days off duty. It was a perfect June day—maybe he would come for her this morning.

Rufus was inclined to be hurt that she hadn't let him know of her trip north to the bedside of her friend. He could have driven her and made the going much easier and pleasanter. But he would come for her at ten and she was to be ready on time. Judith promised not to keep him waiting and went back to her room to find Isabelle and Brenda lying across her bed, shoeless feet dangling.

"Well, it's about time you showed up," Isabelle said as Judith came into the room. "Tell us all about it. She died, didn't she?"

"Yes," Judith replied. "She died the morning after I arrived. I was glad I got there in time."

"I didn't know you had a grandmother, Judy," Brenda said.

"She wasn't really my grandmother," Judith explained. "She called me her 'granddaughter-in-love' and do you know, girls, she left me five thousand dollars in her will. I can't seem to get used to it."

"Wow! Grand!" the girls exclaimed in unison.

"She was a patient of mine during my last year of training in Procton General. She was wonderful to me. I shall miss her. She left something to everyone who worked for her—her nurses, the servants, her doctor and even her lawyer. She must have been wealthy; but one never thought of it while with her."

"I wish one of my patients would show a little appreciation for all the care I shower on them," Isabelle said dolefully. "Look at the years I've been here and the extra time I've spent soothing their woes and calming their fears not to mention the backs I've rubbed which laid end on end would reach from here to Singapore and back."

"What's the idea of changing?" Brenda asked, watching Judith take the white crepe dress from its hanger. "Have you quit this joint now that you've inherited money, Judy? I don't blame you."

"Don't be silly. Winters has given me a couple of days off—she said: 'To recover from the distressing experience through which you have passed.' That's what she said."

Isabelle pretended to swoon while Brenda gasped in astonishment.

"She must have heard you've come into money," Brenda surmised.

"Of course she hasn't heard. No one has heard except you two. I'm not telling it. It's nobody's business. Have you told her you're leaving at the end of the month, Isabelle?" Judith asked, slipping the white dress over her head.

"Not yet. I'm waiting the psychological moment. I want to strike when she least expects it—when she's panning me for some fancied slip of discipline or something. I think she's got an inkling Hank looks me up each time he comes here to the hospital and she doesn't like it. Going out?" she asked as Judith brought out her hat and hung it on one of the bedposts.

"Huh-huh," Judith replied. Then, somewhat defiantly: "I'm going over to the Grant farm. I've promised and promised and now I'm going."

Isabelle left her seat on the bed and came over in her stocking feet to stand before her friend. She put a finger beneath Judith's chin and lifted her face to stare intently into the gray ones. Judith returned the look with one of bland innocence although the color deepened in her cheeks.

"What goes on?" Brenda asked, trying on Judith's white felt hat. "Last I heard Bernice Cranford was dating Rufus Grant—anyway, it's all off with her and Doc Booth."

"Don't mind her, Judy," Isabelle said, noting Judith's sudden stiffening. "The gal's a man-eater. She's not the Grant type—especially after he's known you, darling."

"Just the same, I'd be afraid of her," Brenda declared, replacing the hat and dropping back on the bed. "After all, she is beautiful and she belongs in that crowd."

"Afraid?" Judith asked. "What's there to be afraid of? Rufus and I are just good friends. If Bernice Cranford can get him—why—she's welcome——"

"You don't mean that, Judy Morley," Isabelle rebuked.

"I do," Judith said and tried to make the two little words convincing.

"Well, all I can say is, you're a nut. And by the way, Doc called you last night and was he peeved that you were out of town!" Isabelle kept her eyes on Judith's face as she made the statement.

"Doc? Who? You don't mean Larry Booth?" Judith asked, startled.

"Sure. Who else? It would be just like him to try to gum up the works. I hope that doesn't start again," she muttered more to herself than to Judith.

"What did he want?"

"He didn't tell me, darling. Why should he? He knows how I feel about him. The heel!"

"And Liz Durnford called you, too," Brenda contributed. "Martha has the list of callers, among them several from the Grant man, on a pad somewhere. I declare that girl's the limit. I've told her and told her to put all messages in our rooms but will she do it? Not she. She carries them around in her pocket. Who's Liz Durnford, Judy?"

"Oh, a one-time pal of Larry Booth," Judith said non-committally. "For that matter she's a friend of Rufus Grant, too. I like her. Did she say what she wanted?"

"If she did, Martha didn't mention it," Brenda said. "I'm going to bed. Have yourself a time, Judy, and don't let the cows eat you."

Isabelle lingered. Judith gave her a little shake. "Don't look so worried, Isabelle," she said. "There's no conspiracy afoot that I know of. Liz Durnford has been at the family place somewhere in Maine and no doubt came down for a day or two. She's really a swell person, Isabelle. You'd like her. I believe she's more than a little in love with Larry Booth. She would be fine for him."

"Do you mean that, Judy?" the other asked, earnestly.

"Of course I mean it," Judith said a little impatiently. "What is this, anyway?"

Isabelle Carey put her arm about the smaller girl's shoulders. "It's only that I adore you, Judy," she said softly, "and I want you to be as happy as I am. You'd never be if you took Doctor Booth back."

Judith drew away from the other's affectionate embrace. "What makes you think he wants to be taken back?" she asked quietly.

"He has all the symptoms. Don't do it, Judy. And don't take any stock in the stories about Bernice Cranford and Rufus Grant. The girl's a menace; but Rufus wasn't born yesterday. He's been around and is wise to her little game. Don't let her get you down. Now I, too, am going to bed." She yawned widely. "Hank and I are going over to see how the improvements on the house are coming along. Be seeing you, darling. Have a grand time."

The door closed and Judith sat down before her dressing table to powder her nose. She paused with the puff in her hand to stare at herself in the mirror. Why had Miss Winters given her these two days off? Just what had been the emergency in the Men's Surgical that had cut short her previous rest period? What had Brenda meant by saying Bernice Cranford was dating Rufus?

Suddenly she wished she hadn't telephoned Rufus. Perhaps he had already regretted his statement to Bernice that he and she loved each other. Perhaps he had come to care for Bernice. She laughed mirthlessly.

"Don't be an idiot, Judith Morley," she told the girl in the mirror. "You've been away only four days. People don't change in that short time—but Larry did." The gray eyes reflected in the glass became enormous. She dropped the puff to stare out the window. Suppose Rufus had changed—suppose——She was trembling and got abruptly to her feet.

"Men are born philanderers," Aunt Hepsie had said. "They cause all the misery in the world. Leave 'em alone, Judy. Have no truck with them. They'll lead you on with fine promises and soft words and break your heart in the end. Mark my words—they're all alike."

"But not Rufus, Aunt Hepsie," Judith said and didn't know she spoke aloud.

Ten o'clock. Martha rapped on her door. She handed Judith a folded paper. "Here's the people who 'phoned you, Miss Morley," she said. "I forgot to give it to you before. It don't matter, does it? And that man's here waiting downstairs in the parlor. What'll I tell him this time?"

"You won't have to tell him anything, Martha," Judith said. "I'm going right down. If anyone else calls, tell them I won't be back today or this evening either—until late," she qualified as she saw the girl's eyes widen in interest.

"Where'll I tell 'em you've gone?" Martha asked hopefully.

"You need not tell them. It won't be necessary," Judith said.

Martha sighed and went on down the hall.

"Gosh, I've missed you, Judy," were Rufus Grant's first words as he came to meet her.

"In four days, Rufus? Don't flatter me. I'm not so important as all that," she smiled.

"You are to me. I worried about you."

"You did? That was dear of you; but really there was no need. I was in good hands and I was glad I got there in time. Mrs. Leeds died with her hand in mine—fell asleep. I think I never quite understood that expression before, Rufus. She was very good to me. I shall miss her."

"They tell me she was your grandmother," Rufus said. "I didn't know you had any relatives—I understood——"

"She wasn't my grandmother—not really," Judith explained. "She was a patient of mine during my last year of training in Procton General. We just fell in love with each other. You know, my mother's name was Leeds— Alice Leeds, and we sort of adopted each other for the

176

duration, so to speak, only it has continued ever since. She was a darling, Rufus, and wonderful to me. I feel guilty that I wasn't able to do more for her—give her more of my time. She left me five thousand dollars in her will. I don't deserve it, Rufus."

"I'm sure you do, darling," he contradicted. "The fact she wanted you with her at the last proves she loved you. I'm glad you could be there. It must have been a big help to her."

"She was so sweet——At first I thought I couldn't get away. Miss Winters didn't want to let me go; but Doctor Branch told me to go ahead. He's a peach, Rufus. What I can't understand, though, is why Winters gave me this extra time off. I expected to go right back to work but—well—here I am, having a swell vacation. Isn't it a grand day?"

"Made to order," the man agreed. "We'll get home in time for lunch and then I'll show you the farm. It's a grand place and I know you're going to love it. You see, it's been in the family for five generations. It's lucky for me Andy hated farming, because I love it—couldn't be happy anywhere else. So he took the Nottingham place and the law business and I took the farm. Most of the people on it were there under my father and some of them worked for Grandfather. Matt Wellington's one of them although he was in the Orient for five years after his wife died. But he returned about the time Dad was killed and took over the blacksmith shop again. He's a philosopher. You'll enjoy him—he's a swell old chap."

Judith enjoyed the ride. It was all new country to her, richly fertile. Fine cattle grazed in the rolling meadows, corn, wheat and oats flourished in the fields that stretched for miles. Orchards from which the blossoms had vanished hed promise of a bountiful harvest. Fences zigzagged along the concrete highway. Velvet lawns, dotted with beds of bright flowers, surrounded neat white farmhouses. The occasional raucous clanging of a bell broke the quiet as they purred along beneath wide-spreading maple and chestnut, elm and hickory trees. Traffic was light. A dog ran barking from a driveway only to turn back at a shrill whistle. The car slowed to allow a duck and her brood to waddle across the road or a stupid, fluttery hen. Judith wondered why she had never been this way before. It was delightful and she felt her taut nerves relax and the weariness leave her tired body. How nice to let one's thoughts wander along pleasant bypaths!

"Here's where my land begins," Rufus said after a moment of companionable silence in which the two in the car seemed to draw closer together in spirit. "We come to the house in a few minutes—about a mile farther on. Nice country around here—best in the State—we believe. Do you ride, Judy?"

"No, Rufus. I'm sorry," she said and meant it. "I've never been on a horse in my life. Why, does it matter?"

"Of course not. You'll learn in no time. We can get around the farm more quickly on horseback than on foot. Then, too, there are some awkward trails out here where a car can't go—a horse can. We'll have to see about a horse for you, Judy."

Judith said nothing. She would just pretend this one day anyway. She didn't feel like arguing—she has exhausted her arguments. There was nothing left. It seemed to her Rufus was the most determined person she had ever known and, she told herself with wonder and something like resignation, that she loved him with all her heart.

"Don't refuse happiness, Judith—grasp it with both hands—nourish it—be grateful."

It seemed to her that Mrs. Leeds' gentle voice spoke to her. Her eyes filled with sudden tears and she winked rapidly to prevent their falling.

The house was of gray stone. It looked very old. Vines clambered over one side running to the very tops of the tall broad chimneys. The wide front veranda was cool and inviting with its gay striped awnings and wicker furnishings. The spacious lawns were green velvet. Huge elms towered above the house and made a colonnade from the highway to the front door. Big and sprawling and rather overwhelming but homey and inviting in spite of its size.

Rufus parked the car in the side yard and they walked to the front steps. A red Irish setter rose lazily from his place in the shade and trotted to meet them, wagging a friendly tail. There was a mad barking and yapping from the hall inside and a bundle of white fur dashed itself against the screen door.

"That's Patsy," Rufus explained, "and this is Mark Anthony. Mark is getting old," he added pulling the setter's silky ears.

"Hello, Mark," Judy murmured, patting the dog's head. He nestled against her and Rufus grinned.

"He's the most affectionate animal I ever saw. Thinks he's a lap dog. Wait till you sit down. He'll want to climb into your lap. He's like that if he takes to anyone. Sometimes he doesn't and then look out."

They mounted the shallow steps and Rufus rang the bell. The housekeeper answered. Mrs. Jeffrey was a stout, motherly woman, frankly middle-aged and comfortable. With the vociferous Patsy held firmly under one arm, she greeted Judith with friendly warmth, ushering her to a room at the top of the long winding stairs, where she urged her "to lay off your hat and gloves and make yourself at home."

"Come down when you feel like it, my dear," she said as she left. "Rufus will be in the library, no doubt, looking over the mail. There's a pile of it this morning."

Judith remained in her room for some time. From the rear window she could see the garden with its masses of flowers, the water from a fountain flashing in the sun. A huge oak towered above a white semi-circular seat, a table before it. A sundial stood in an open space and the gleam from a sizable pool was visible through the trees. Off to the right were the tennis courts, while beyond a path led to a clump of birches, their white trunks and silvery leaves making Judith catch her breath in delight. She supposed

179

the barns, garage and stables were on the other side. Nothing obscured the view from these windows. Perhaps this was one of the guest rooms. She turned her eyes to examine the room. Without doubt everything in it was at least a hundred years old—except, perhaps, the draperies and linen, and even they carried out the ideas of another day. She sat down before the quaint dressing-table and smoothed her hair. She wondered how many girls had sat there and did just what she was doing, while a Grant in the library below awaited her return, for she was sure Rufus was doing just that. Suddenly she felt shy. By coming here it seemed as if she had capitulated. But had she? Could she put the past completely behind her—live in the present and future? Or was this visit to result in greater unhappiness for her?

"You're afraid of love, my dear. Afraid to follow your heart."

She slid off the seat and stood erect, her back to the mirror, her head high.

"Today I'm going to be happy, Aunt Hepsie," she silently informed her invisible Nemesis. "I'm not a coward. I can bear whatever comes. I'm strong; but I've got to have this little slice of happiness."

Chin up and a smile on her lips, she slowly descended the stairs. As if he had sensed her coming, Rufus was standing in the hall below.

CHAPTER FIFTEEN

I THOUGHT you were taking a nap, Judy," Rufus greeted his guest as she joined him at the foot of the stairs. "I was just accidentally on purpose going to make a racket outside your window. This is my day, darling, and I want every minute of it."

"Why, that's the very idea I had, Rufus," Judith smiled. "I was thinking that today I'm going to forget the hospital and everything unpleasant and unhappy and be glad to be here—to be alive and young and healthy."

"Atta girl," he applauded. "First, we'll have lunch and then I'll take you on a tour of inspection. I want you to meet my people—I'm sure you'll like them and I know they'll all fall in love with you. Let's pretend I've brought you here to live, Judy—a bride—and you're getting acquainted with *your* people——"

"How old are you, Rufus?" Judith teased.

"Today I feel like a boy. I've tried so hard to get you out here and now that I've actually succeeded, it has gone to my head. Come on, darling, let's eat and then we'll go."

The luncheon was delicious and Judith ate slowly, dreamily, savoring each morsel to its fullest value while her host regaled her with tales of the house, the horses, the people who lived on the estate. Judith was amazed at the historical background and felt her heart sink as she realized anew the difference in their stations. He seemed to sense her reaction and hastened to change the atmosphere.

"Oh, there were a few rotten apples on the family tree, Judy. A few blackguards among the Grants," he told her. "What old family hasn't had a couple of black sheep within its fold at some time or another; but they didn't seem to taint the rest. As a whole, the Grants have been pretty fair. We've never been saints but most of us have been decent. That's something, isn't it? I'll show you some of their portraits a bit later and let you judge for yourself."

Judith put down her napkin. "Everything was delicious, Rufus. I don't think I ever enjoyed a meal more thoroughly

—especially the entertainment. Do you know, my friend, you're a very lucky man."

"I am *now*, Judy," he said seriously. "With you sitting opposite; the sun shining on your hair; your lovely eyes serene and even happy, I feel I'm the luckiest chap in all the world. When you come here to remain beside me permanently, I'll never forget to thank God for giving me such happiness. That's a promise, Judy."

Judith's eyes were misty as they looked into his. "You're sweet, Rufus," she murmured. "I wish——"

A maid came to tell Rufus he was wanted on the telephone. "You stopped just there once before, Judy," he said as he excused himself and went into the next room.

What was it she wished? Judith knew but felt it was providential that each time she was about to put that wish into words, there had come an interruption. She must not get any deeper.

When Rufus returned, he seemed to have forgotten Judith's unexpressed wish and they left the house on a tour of the farm. First to the stables where the riding horses were kept. The groom was only too proud to display his charges to Judith, who had never in her life touched a horse, smoothed the satin head and neck of a small mare while the animal whinnied in delight. Rufus beamed.

"We'll make a horsewoman of you yet, my dear," he told her as they walked down the path to the blacksmith shop. "Listen to Matt singing. He has the most wonderful disposition of any man I know. A grand guy if there ever was one. He was here in my grandfather's day. His wife died before he was mustered out of the last war. He never got over it."

A huge man stood with his back to them. In the comparative gloom of the shop, the forge glowed red and with every clang of the hammer on the anvil, the deep resonant voice roared out in greater volume. Judith couldn't understand the words—perhaps they were foreign; but the tune was rollicking and the rhythmic motions of the smith reminded her of the conductor of some symphony—in fact, it was a symphony. They stood just inside watching and listening until the job in hand was completed. The song ceased and the big man turned. Judith thought she had never seen a more wonderful face. Strong and kind and experienced.

"Oh, hello, Rufus!" he greeted his employer. "Making quite a racket, wasn't I? Sorry."

"That's all right, Matt," Rufus said cordialy. "I brought Judy down to see you—I want you to know each other."

"Howdy, Miss," the man said, offering his hand then drawing it back. "I'm afraid I'm a mess. Consider your hand shaken."

"Indeed I shall not, Mr.—Matt," Judith said, holding out her hand. "I want to shake hands with you. Please."

The big man grinned at her. "All right, lady. The result be upon your own head—hand." But Judith knew he was pleased. "What did Rufus call you?" he asked.

"Judy," the girl told him. "My name is Judith—Judith Morley."

"Good name," the man murmured, his eyes appreciating her fresh young beauty. "Fitting, too, I'd say."

Judith smiled. "Sometimes I think it doesn't fit at all —that it's too big for me. Perhaps Judy is better."

"Because you are small in stature? Ah, but it isn't the outside wrappings that matter. Sometimes the bulkiest packages contain nothing but trash. It's what's inside that counts—a stout heart—a courageous spirit that makes a person big in spite of his physical size. Let me see, seems as though Rufus told me you're a nurse. Right?"

"Right," Judith agreed. So Rufus had discussed her with this friendly yet dignified man. Somehow it made her feel as if she knew him—as if he even approved of her. It had a steadying effect on her.

"Like it?"

"Yes—most times."

"Intend sticking to it?"

Judith looked from him to Rufus. Just how much did he know about her? "I—I——" she began.

183

"Not if I can make her realize she is needed here, Matt," Rufus interrupted. "We need her, don't we?" he asked.

Matt said nothing for a moment as he stared through the open door into the bright sunshine that flooded the world with light.

"Every home needs a woman in it," he said softly. I know, for my own house hasn't been a home since Trudie died. Mind telling me just why you hesitate or is it none of my business—to your way of thinking? You see, I helped bring Rufus up—made a pretty good job of it, too. Even when I was over across on the other side of the world I kept tabs on him. Like nursing strangers better than you would your own family?"

Somehow it didn't seem at all peculiar that he should be talking to her so. His manner toward Rufus was indeed more like that of a father than an employee. She looked into his kind eyes and a torrent of words poured from her lips.

"I don't know whether or not Rufus has told you; but I am of a different world—my people were poor, desperately poor. The aunt who brought me up impressed upon me the fact that a curse followed the women of our family—that happiness was not for me. My father disappeared before I was born. My mother was killed under the most unhappy circumstances. I'm not even sure my name is my own although the records show my mother married Jude Morley; but Aunt Hepsie insisted it was not his real name—that he probably had a wife and family somewhere else. Now you know. What can I do?" She paused; her eyes were dark and tragic in her dead white face.

Rufus laid an arm across her shoulders, but she drew back from his embrace to stand apart.

"But, child," Matt reminded her, "that's all past. There's nothing you can help or alter. None of this concerns the present or the future."

"How can you say that? It does," the girl cried. "Can't you see that it does?"

"No," It was said emphatically. "It's your pride speaking, not your heart. Why not follow your heart for a change?"

There it was again. "Follow your heart—take hold of happiness with both hands—nourish it—guard it with your life."

Judith covered her face with her hands. Rufus caught her to him. "There, there, darling," he crooned against her hair. "We'll not pester you any more. If you don't want to marry me—you—don't have to——"

"But I do," wailed Judith, burrowing her head into his shoulder. "Oh, I do—you know I do!"

"Then do it!" shouted Matt. " 'Let the dead past bury its dead,' as the poet sings. 'Rise on the stepping-stones' of all that past unhappiness to greater glory in the future. By godfrey, girl, why do you persist in torturing yourself with a lot of superstitions—a lot of hokum some loony old woman filled your infant mind with? If you had been older it would have all run off like water off a duck; but likely you were just young enough to have it all sink in and stick. However, you're a big girl now—an adult. Why not act your age?"

Rufus chuckled and Judith turned a suddenly smiling but tear-stained face toward the indignant old man. "That's telling me," she said. "I wish Aunt Hespie could have heard you."

"I wish to heaven she had—maybe she hears me now wherever she is. I certainly hope so. Of all the utterly diabolic tricks ever perpetrated against a youngster I believe that was the worst yet. The wonder is that you got through as well as you did. Well, now that you seem to have come to your senses, when are you two getting married?"

"O-oh!" breathed Judith.

"Soon," Rufus said firmly, holding her close.

"I second the boy's motion," Matt said. "He needs you, Judith. Be kind to him—love him a great deal—he's worthy of your confidence. You see, I know him.

Now I've got a little trinket over in my box I'd like you to have, my dear," he went on after a moment. "It's a talisman given me by an old Chinese friend I have in the Orient." He joined in the laugh of his two visitors. "And here I was scolding about an old woman's voodoo; but just the same it's pretty and quite valuable—or so Li Wong said. Wait here and I'll fetch it."

"You mean it, darling, don't you?" Rufus asked when the old man had disappeared. "You won't let me down again." He pressed his cheek to hers.

"It's strange," the girl said wonderingly, "but ever since I was with Mrs. Leeds last week things have seemed different—the past has become more remote—less forbidding. Somehow I wasn't afraid any longer."

"Afraid, darling? But why?"

Judith shook her head. "That's it. I don't know why. I just was. It was nothing tangible—nothing I could put my finger on—I felt as Damocles must have—any moment the sword might drop, and sometimes I wished it would and put an end to the suspense. Perhaps I should have consulted a psychiatrist long ago." She raised her head and threw her arms wide. "I feel free!" she cried. "Oh, Rufus, it's wonderful!"

"Here you are, my dear," Matt said, coming into the shop. He held out a small pale green object. Judith stared, then put out her hand almost fearfully.

"A willow whistle!" she whispered.

"Not willow, Judith," Matt explained. "Jade. You know jade is believed to cure pain. This particular trinket has the added virtues of promoting happiness and providing protection against evil spirits as well, or so my Chinese friend informed me. Why do you look so—well—strange, my dear?"

"It is very queer," the girl said in a tone almost of awe, "but you see, the only thing I had belonging to my father were two willow whistles my mother brought with her when she came to my aunt's before I was born. He used to whittle them from willow twigs. My aunt burned them while I was still only a baby. It—it seems almost like a—like a sign———"

"Maybe it is," Matt told her. "If it's any comfort to you to think so I guess there's no harm in it. Who can say for sure, anyway?"

"I shall treasure it always, Matt. Thank you."

"You've got company, Rufus," the old man said, slightly embarrassed at Judith's gratitude. "I almost forgot to tell you what with this and the other thing. I saw a station wagon come up the avenue just as I came in."

Judith seemed not to have heard. She was turning the jade whistle over and over in her hands, her thoughts trying to pierce the veil separating the two worlds. Were her father and mother together again? Was this a sign that Aunt Hespie had been wrong in her teaching? That in reality only a few men were blackguards and villains—that actually most of them were decent and good, worthy of a girl's devotion? Aunt Hepsie, who had been the most vivid of all Judith's memories, began to recede into the limbo of other unhappy and disagreeable things.

"What rotten luck!" Rufus complained as he pulled Judith's hand through his arm. "Well, we'll have to go back to the house. Keep your fingers crossed, darling. We'll make short work of whoever has the temerity to break into our privacy. Oh, it's heavenly having you all to myself, Judy! Do you feel it?"

"Yes," Judith said happily. "I shall always love this place. Please don't think I'm silly, Rufus, but I seem to have found my father and mother—they—well, they have always appeared so shadowy and unreal to me but suddenly they are real—people I can love and honor even if they are no longer alive. Oh, you don't know what it means to me. I feel light—as if I had been very ill or blind and had recovered health and sight. It began when Mrs. Leeds talked to me as she was dying—Matt completed the cure. A weight has been lifted from my heart. I don't know how to express it—but—but I'm happy, Rufus, and—o-oh!" she exclaimed, stopping in her tracks. "Isn't that

Bernice Cranford there by the station wagon? And who is——Why, it's Liz Durnford, too."

Rufus frowned and his voice was anything but cordial as he muttered. "What the deuce are they doing here—today of all days? Bernice threatened to drop in on me some day but I hoped she would forget it. Well, I suppose there's nothing we can do about it as long as they're here. Let's get rid of them as quickly as possible."

"Hi!" Liz shouted when she caught sight of them.

Bernice Cranford turned and stared in unbelief as she recognized Judith. She and Liz walked down the path to meet them.

"Fancy seeing you here, Judy!" Liz said cordially as they approached. "This is going to be a real party—one hundred per cent surprise. How's Larry? Working hard, I suppose?"

Judith nodded, her throat stiff. She felt the antagonism of Bernice engulf her and wondered how she was to combat it. Her fingers tightened on the jade whistle and suddenly her confidence returned. They reached the porch and Rufus said:

"I'll see about something cold in the way of refreshment, girls," and left them. Judith felt deserted. Liz smiled wisely.

"Lovely place you have here, my dear."

"We like it," Judith said and felt a little gurgle of laughter welling up inside her.

"We?" Bernice asked. "Who may we be?"

"Don't be a goon, Bernice," Liz said, slipping over to sit on the arm of Judith's chair. "I saw it coming, old girl," she whispered.

Bernice kept her eyes straight ahead. Her face was flushed and her chin set in stubborn lines. "You know Larry Booth and I are no longer engaged, don't you?" she said at last, not looking at Judith.

"Why no," Judith answered. "I'm sorry. He seemed so happy and I thought—I understood the wedding was to be soon."

"Well, it isn't. Catch me tying myself to a doctor. They're machines—live and eat and breathe hospital—operation—emergency. Not for me, thank you."

"I'm sorry," Judith said again.

"I don't know why you should be," the other snapped, then apologized. "I'm sorry."

"Better to find it out before the march up the aisle," Liz said, "than after. Larry's too fine a man to get a raw deal like that."

Judith recalled the drive back from the accident on the night of the Appletree Inn dance when Larry had muttered: "I've been a damned fool!" Had he, too, found that his engagement to the chief's granddaughter was a mistake?

"I thought you and he were that way about each other before I appeared upon the scene, Judy," Bernice said, turning to look at the girl sitting quietly in the chair opposite.

"Larry and I were always friends," Judith said serenely and felt a great contentment that she could say it honestly and without guile. She felt rather than saw Rufus return to the porch. He stood in the doorway close beside her chair. A maid came out with a tray and he motioned her to place it on the table nearby. When the screen door closed behind her he turned to Bernice.

"When are you and Doctor Booth middle-aisling it, Bernice?" he asked, although Judith knew Bernice had told him the engagement was broken.

"Never," the girl said shortly. "I told you it was off and I meant it. I'll have no divided allegiance."

Judith caught her breath. What was she wanting to imply? Liz laughed and eased the tension.

"I can see you'll never make a successful doctor's wife, Bernice," she told her. "They have to come in contact with too many women—and nurses." She winked at Judith who shook her head.

"Well," said Rufus firmly, his arms lifting Judith from her chair to his side where he held her close, "here's one nurse he'll not come into contact with—much longer, Bernice."

"O-oh," Bernice said slowly, "so it's that way with you?"

"I think I mentioned it some time ago, didn't I?" he reminded her. "The day we had our hair down and were telling each other things. Remember?"

Liz ran to them and threw her arms about them both. "You dear things!" she cried ecstatically. "I saw it coming—'way back when you held hands in the movies—remember? You thought I was so wrapped up in Larry I didn't know what was going on right under my nose, didn't you? Congratulations, darlings! You were made for each other if ever two people were." She kissed Judith and pulled Rufus' face down to hers and kissed him, too.

Bernice got to her feet slowly as if reluctant to do so. She held out her hands to her hosts. "I think it's wonderful," she said and if it was said with an effort, the two most concerned refused to notice it. "I'm leaving for the coast early next week," she went on more briskly; then— "No doubt you think me pretty much a heel, Judith Morley," she said, "and I guess I'm a spoiled brat at that. My grandfather was right when he told me I should have been spanked often and soundly when I was a child. But just the same, I do wish you both every happiness."

"Thank you, Bernice," she said softly, "and I wish for you all the happiness in the world."

"And now that all this is out of the way, suppose we have that cold drink you promised us, Rufus," Liz, suggested, turning to the table on which a pitcher and glasses stood. "Let's drink to your future—and the future of us all." She held her glass high. "Here's to us," she misquoted, "there's nobody like us and nobody likes us better than we do ourselves!"

"That's rank heresy, Liz," Rufus protested, "and, anyway, it's no way to toast a prospective bride and groom. Can't you do better than that?"

"Sure, I can. How's this? Here's to the sweetest girl and finest boy in the world—long may they love!"

"That's some better, but even that isn't up to your usual form," Rufus told her.

"Well, I'm getting out of here," Bernice announced. "I have an appointment at four and I promised Grandmother to go calling with her. Coming, Liz?"

Within the circle of Rufus' arm Judith watched the station wagon down the drive and out into the highway. She waved good-bye and turned to bury her face in the shoulders hollowed to receive it. Rufus held her close for a moment.

"You were wonderful, darling," he whispered. "I'm proud of you!"

Silence for a space, then Judith lifted glowing eyes to his. "Do you know, Rufus, I'd like to go back to Niles Corners again. I should like to visit Doctor Wales. Isn't it strange how everything has straightened out—the past is all dim and lovely now—all the rought spots and ugly happenings seem not to matter."

"I'm glad," Rufus said. He pressed the hand holding the jade whistle to his lips. "I'm glad it's all washed up—that you'll never again be haunted by ghosts from the past; but let me tell you, darling, love like mine can overcome any kind of an obstacle and I believe in time it would have melted even your stony heart even without your grand-mother-in-love, old Matt, or the jade whistle." His voice roughened. "Come to me soon, Judy," he begged. "I want you here with me. Don't keep me waiting long, darling."

"Isabelle wanted me to consent to a double wedding, Rufus," she smiled. "I laughed at her. I wasn't at all sure I should capitulate so quickly and completely."

"When is she getting married?" he asked excitedly. "Why can't we do it at the same time—if it's soon?"

"Oh, no," Judith cried. "Why she's being married at once—on the last day of June—at the minister's house!"

"Well—let's do it, darling. Cut all the fuss and bother and I'll take you away for a long holiday and then we'll come home—home, Judy!" he whispered. "Are you going to love it here—even as I do?"

"Who could help it? But I still think the last day of June is too soon. Why I didn't even know I could marry you until just a little while ago," she temporized. "I think, perhaps, the fall would be quite enough under the circumstances."

"Listen, Judith," Rufus said seriously. "If we get into this war—and there is every indication that we shall—I'm going. I want to know you are here waiting for me—praying for me—loving me. Things happen so quickly—don't you see, darling? Marry me at once—just as soon as it can be arranged. I love you!" he whispered against her lips.

"All right, Rufus," she said, clinging to him. "I'll marry you any time you say. I love you."

She felt his tumultuous heartbeat beneath her cheek and pressed closer within his arms. Oh, it was wonderful to stand like this—to feel his nearness—to know he belonged to her as she did to him—for always! She sensed again the jade whistle in her hand and drew back from his embrace to lift it to her lips. From it came a long, eerie sound, thin and penetrating. The breeze carried it away and away.

Down in the blacksmith shop, an old man raised his head to stare back across the years. Once he had been young and in love and the girl he held in his arms was as beautiful as the one Rufus would bring to the farm as his wife.

"Good luck to you, son!" he said aloud, waving a hand in the direction of the house. "And to you, Judith. May life be kind to you and health and happiness be your portion. Love," he whispered, "it's still the greatest thing in the world!"

He picked up a horseshoe and went to work. His voice lifted in song, its rollicking tones spilling out from the shop and echoing through the trees. Back on the porch a man and girl smiled into each other's eyes.

THE END